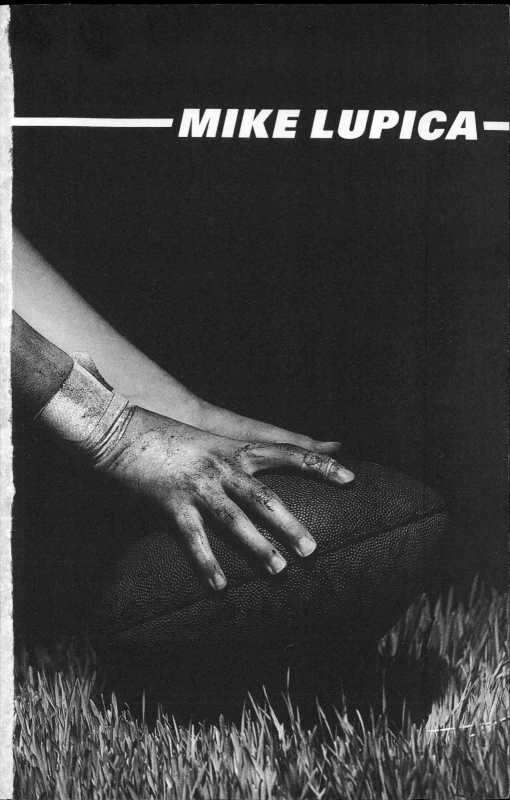

MIKE LUPICA

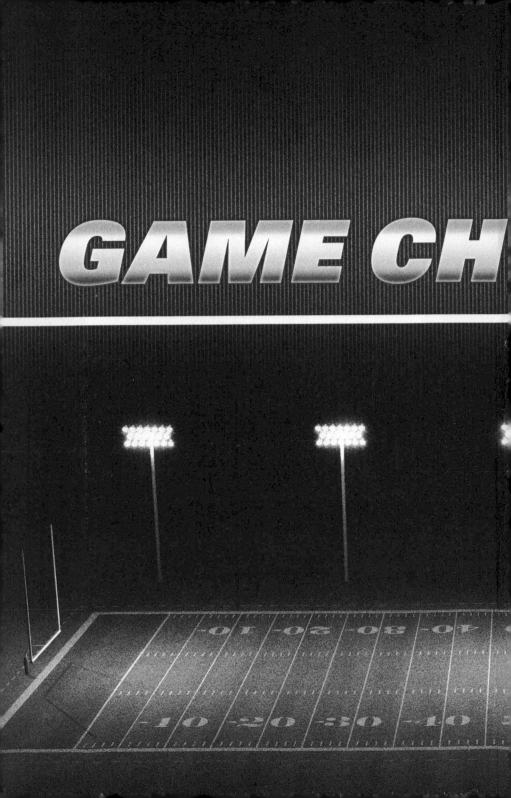

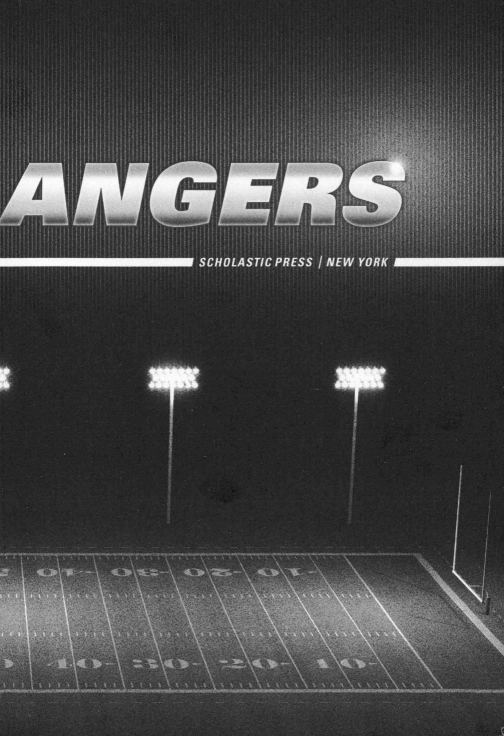

ANGERS

SCHOLASTIC PRESS | NEW YORK

Library of Congress Cataloging-in-Publication Data Available

ISBN 978-0-545-38182-6

12 11 10 9 8 7 6 5 4 3 2 1   12 13 14 15 16/0

Printed in the U.S.A. 23

First edition, June 2012

Book design by Phil Falco

For my mother and father.

*And for the great Doug Flutie of Boston College,
No. 22, who was supposed to be too small, and
still became a giant of college football.*

BOOKS BY
MIKE LUPICA

Ben McBain, eleven years old and nowhere near five feet tall, had always thought of himself as a quarterback even though most grown-ups didn't see it that way.

Mostly the grown-ups who had coached him in football so far.

It was because they thought he was too small to play quarterback. He got that. He did. Got that he didn't look the part, didn't look like a quarterback to them, even the ones who had actually taken the time to notice the way he could throw a football before they told him he was going to play another position.

Running back.

Wide receiver.

Kick returner.

Just never quarterback.

He kept trying, every season. But somebody else always beat him out. Two years ago it had been Steven Moore, before he moved out of Rockwell. Last year it was Shawn O'Brien when his family moved *back* to Rockwell.

Both bigger. By a lot.

Both looking the part.

Ben knew in his heart that he had all the skills needed to be a quarterback, not just the arm. More than that, he knew he had the ability to do the one thing that was supposed to count the most in sports:

The ability to make a play.

It always came down to that, whether you were playing in the schoolyard at Rockwell Middle School at recess, or in the small park across the street from your house, or even on the real football field behind their school, the field they all called The Rock.

Ben still thought of himself as a quarterback even knowing he was barely big enough to play *any* position in Pop Warner football, that he was just going to make the minimum require-ment for weight this season in the Midget Division of the Butler County League for eleven-year-olds.

The limit was one hundred pounds. Ben was one hundred and one, he weighed himself every morning to make sure he hadn't dropped a couple while he was sleeping.

Sometimes he couldn't help himself, he imagined they'd named the division for him, that *he* was going to be the midget on his team and in their league.

But when he'd say something like that to his dad, Jeff McBain would look at him and say, "So play bigger, big boy."

"When it's football season," Ben said, "I just want to *be*

bigger."

Of course his dad was 6-2 and weighed two hundred pounds, which is what he'd weighed when he'd been a defensive back at Boston College. It was Ben's mom who was the small one, about 5-2 and half his dad's weight. The family pediatrician, Dr. Freshman, had done all these projections and said that Ben might grow to be 5-8 someday. Probably not more than that.

Making it sound like a good thing. His father liked to joke that Ben lucked out getting his mother's looks, but he got her short legs, too.

Size didn't bother Ben in the other sports he played. It didn't. Didn't hold him back or slow him down. He was a pitcher in baseball when he wasn't playing just about every other position on the field, even catcher sometimes, though catching equipment seemed to swallow him up the way pads and his helmet did in football. He was a point guard in basketball who could pass like a pro and already knew how to create enough space to get his shot when he wasn't beating guys off the dribble with his speed.

And he could always beat people with his speed in football, no worries there, could do that carrying the ball from the backfield or catching it or returning punts and kickoffs.

But there wasn't a single day he'd ever played Pop Warner, from the time he started playing in the third grade, that he didn't think he was playing out of position.

"I'm trying out for quarterback again," Ben had said to his dad in the car on the way to tryouts.

"There's a shocker," his dad had said.

"I won't get it," Ben had said.

"You don't know that before the tryouts even start."

"Yeah, Dad, I do."

His dad had dropped him off behind Rockwell Middle School and left, because none of the parents were allowed to watch the tryouts, it was a league rule, only the coach and the three evaluators from the town football committee were allowed to be there. So Ben was on the field now with three dozen kids who'd been separated right away by position. When they asked who wanted to try out for quarterback, only three raised their hands: Shawn O'Brien, Ben, and a new kid in their grade, Barry Stanton.

Ben had watched Barry warm up, saw he had a decent enough arm. But he was going to have no chance to beat out Shawn. Shawn O'Brien was trying out tonight the way everybody else at The Rock was. But by next week, when real practices started, he was going to be the starter the way he was last season, the way he probably would be all the way through Rockwell High School.

He wasn't always consistent, was more like a streak shooter in basketball. Last season he'd have these streaks where he couldn't miss, even though they didn't come so often the second half of the season. But when he would get on one of those rips, showing off his arm, it was all anybody wanted to talk about when the game was over.

Now Ben knew there was no point in saying the job was Shawn's to lose, because he wasn't losing it.

Shawn had it all. He was big enough to be a tight end, he could run like a wide receiver in the open field, he was strong enough to shake off tacklers, he had that strong arm going for him.

And if that wasn't enough, Shawn had one other thing going for him that no one else at The Rock had:

He was the coach's son, his dad coaching him this season for the first time.

Ben hoped it would make Shawn O'Brien easier to be around. Last year he had been too much of a hothead, had seemed stuck-up to Ben and Sam Brown and Coop Manley — his best buds — and just about everybody else on the team. Sometimes the only talking he did to the other players at practice was calling the signals. And if somebody made a mistake on him, missed a block or dropped a pass, he had this way of acting as if the kid who did it had stolen his lunch money.

Maybe he was going to change now that his dad was around. Sam didn't think so, had decided that Shawn was going to be more of a knucklehead than ever, said there was always a different set of rules for a coach's son, even if coaching dads never seemed to realize that.

"Guys always say it's tough to have to play for their dad," Sam said. "Dude, you know better than that."

And it wasn't as if Matt O'Brien was just *any* coach. He was the best football player to ever come out of Rockwell, had gone on from Rockwell High to being a college star at Maryland, that he'd even spent a couple of seasons backing up Peyton Manning with the Colts. *Everybody* in town knew about all that.

Matt O'Brien had moved back to Rockwell the year before last, in the process of selling a chain of restaurants he'd started after he left the NFL. According to Ben's dad, Mr.

O'Brien ended up making such an insane amount of money in the deal he decided to retire. He was still too busy with the sale to coach last year's team. But when he offered to coach the Midget Division team this season, the people running town football acted like Peyton Manning himself had applied for the job of coaching the Rockwell Rams.

It was perfect, if you weren't trying to beat Shawn out of a job. The dad had been a quarterback. The son was a quarterback. Like *that* was their real family business.

Ben still had to try out.

"Of course you're trying out, you wouldn't be you if you *didn't* try," his friend Lily had said to him at school that day.

So Ben was trying as hard as he ever had at the end of the first night of tryouts, finally his turn to play quarterback against a real defense. Shawn had already had his turn, making all his throws, running for a first down when he got flushed out of the pocket one time, only muffing one exchange with a running back. So maybe you gave him an A- instead of an A.

Now it was Ben's first shot at making this year's coach see a quarterback instead of the littlest guy on the field, one hundred and one pounds exactly.

Only Ben's first play had turned into a busted play. It was why he was running hard to his right now, being chased by what felt like half the players Coach O'Brien had lined up to stop him.

Ben was always the star of schoolyard football — "greatest recess QB ever," Sam liked to say — and it felt like the first night of tryouts had turned into schoolyard football now.

Ben buying himself some time and trying to make a play, even if it wasn't exactly the one Coach had called for him in the huddle.

It was supposed to be a simple buttonhook to Sam, the best and fastest receiver on the field behind Rockwell Middle School, and the one with the surest hands.

Sam was supposed to take off like it was a straight fly pattern, stop, and come back for the ball. If he ran the pattern right and Ben delivered the ball, the play would be a solid ten-yard completion. Or more, if Sam broke a tackle.

Only when Sam came back for the ball the middle linebacker, Justin Bard, was sitting there like a big old crow on a fence.

No chance to get the ball past him. No time for Ben to dump the ball off to his receiver over in the left flat.

And no fun in that, anyway.

Go big or go home, Ben thought to himself.

When he ran out of room at the right sideline, Ben was the one who came to a sudden stop now, spun around, back to the action, running toward the middle of the field. Looking *down*field the first chance he got, his eyes trying to pick up where Sam was.

But after all the football they'd played together in their lives, Sam Brown had picked *him* up. He was running in the same direction Ben was, like they were on parallel train tracks, waiting to see what Ben's next move was going to be, knowing that was always the fun of being on Ben McBain's team:

Finding out what was going to happen next.

So Sam probably wasn't blown away when he saw Ben reverse his field again, running *back* toward the sideline. He could throw a ball just fine running to his left. But he was right-handed. When he really wanted to put something extra on the ball, wanted to bring the heat and go deep, he was better moving to his right.

Sam took off down the field then.

Ben gave one last quick look over his shoulder, just to make sure nobody was gaining on him. They weren't, because they were running out of steam now, tired of chasing.

Ben set himself and let the ball go.

Not throwing it as far as he could because he didn't need to throw it that far. Just putting it in Sam's hands when he was clear of the cornerback covering him, watching as Sam caught the ball at the five-yard line and breezed into the end zone from there.

Coop, the center who'd snapped Ben the ball what felt like about twenty minutes ago, came over to stand next to Ben, casually high-fived him.

Then Coop — whose real first name was Cooper — tipped his helmet back and grinned. "That's what *I'm* talkin' about."

"Just the way we drew it up," Ben said, grinning back at him.

"Yeah," Coop said, "if we were playing Angry Birds."

The other guys trying out for quarterback had made some good plays tonight. Some great throws. Just not like this one. Not off the kind of busted play that Ben had turned into pure money.

It was why Ben couldn't help himself now, had to steal a look over at Coach, see what his reaction was.

Only there wasn't one.

Coach O'Brien was over on the sideline, back turned, showing Shawn the proper way to pivot away from center and make the handoff he'd messed up earlier.

Coop saw where Ben was looking.

"He didn't see," Coop said.

"They never do," Ben said.

The park across the street from where Ben lived in Rockwell had always been like his own private playground.

His dad said that technically the town owned it, and that it had been much bigger when he was a boy, before an even bigger park was built closer to the center of Rockwell. But the grass still got mowed, and there was still a swing set and see-saw at the far end where moms would bring small kids, a small basketball court with one hoop, and beyond that a place where people could walk their dogs.

Ben's buds called it "McBain Field," just because he always seemed to be out there. And if you didn't mind playing football with swing sets behind one end zone and some hedges at the other — and on a field that wasn't much wider than a two-lane road — you could have a decent game of touch.

Three-on-three was the best. If you went with more players than that, you could sometimes feel as if you were trying to get open in your own bedroom.

But three-on-three worked fine, had just worked for Ben and some of the guys on this Saturday morning at McBain

Field. Ben and Sam and Coop on one team. Justin Bard and the Clayton brothers, Darrelle and Rodney, on the other. All guys from the Pop Warner team.

They had been playing all morning, only stopping now because the Claytons had to go visit some relatives a couple of towns over with their parents, entering what Darrelle always called a "no-fun zone." Justin had to leave, too, for his guitar lesson.

So it was Ben, Sam, and Coop stretched out on the grass. Lily Wyatt was there with them, having just ridden her bike from her house two blocks over.

No one had told Lily the game was ending, it was as if she had some sixth sense going for her. Ben used to think it was just him, Lily being able to hack into his brain the way people said they could hack into computers. But the more time they spent together — and it was a lot, their moms were best friends, and Ben and Lily had been born a month apart — Ben had just decided that Lily Wyatt just knew a lot of stuff that other kids their age didn't.

Like she was eleven going on thirty.

She wasn't cocky, never a show-off in any way. She was too cool for that. In class she'd let other kids come up with answers even though Ben suspected she knew every one as soon as a teacher had finished asking the question. There was this look she'd give Ben, just for his benefit. This smile she had that told him she was always a couple of moves ahead of him, and that he shouldn't even bother trying to catch up.

Lily could also handle herself around Ben's guy friends like a champ. Going back to when they all started school together, neither Sam nor Coop had ever complained about having a girl be part of their pack.

When it came to baseball Ben and Sam were both Red Sox fans. Coop was the Yankee fan in the group, knew all about them, knew that a few years ago four of their veterans — Derek Jeter, Mariano Rivera, Jorge Posada, Andy Pettitte — were known as the "Core Four." It was why he had always called Ben, Sam, Lily, and him the Core Four.

Now the four of them were sitting underneath the maple tree at the side of the park closest to Ben's house, the four of them needing the shade on a September afternoon that felt like the middle of summer, the temperature today over ninety degrees.

They were talking about the same thing they had been talking about all week: The football tryouts, and the fact that even though Ben had played as well as Shawn every time they had scrimmaged, Coach O'Brien had officially named Shawn the starting quarterback the night before. Ben was going to get time at halfback, wide receiver, and return kicks, same as last year.

Same old, same old.

They'd all gotten the same list from Coach the night before, the twenty-nine players who had made it through the whole week. They'd started with three dozen kids, but a few had quit by Friday.

"At least you tried," Lily said to Ben now. "Think how much worse you'd feel about yourself if you didn't."

"Yeah," Ben said. "I can't believe how much better that makes me feel."

Sam said, "Who was it that said there are no medals for trying?"

Lily said, "Somebody's parent, probably."

"Or a coach," Sam said. "Like the guy who said that winning isn't everything, it's the only thing."

"How dumb is that, by the way?" Lily said. "You mean sports can't be fun if you lose?"

"Well, it *is* more fun if you win," Ben said. "And that includes winning the job you want."

"Dude," Sam said, "you know you're gonna have fun this season whether you're the QB or not." Pausing before adding, "Even though you should be the QB."

Stubborn to the end.

"You ever gonna let that go?" Coop said to Sam.

"Do I ever let go of the ball once I've got it?" Sam said.

Coop said, "Dude, the good news is that Coach wants to have the ball in Ben's hands as much as possible. And we've got a chance to win the league. What more do you want?"

"Our best quarterback to play quarterback," Sam said. "And Ben's our best."

Lily smiled. "Well, at least the best son won."

"Aw, man," Coop said, "I wish I'd said that."

Sam still wasn't done.

"Coaches always tell you that they're gonna play the best guys," Sam said. Really dug in now. "And that's gonna be true this season for every position on the field except the most important one. Everybody saw what you did all week except the guy who *should* have seen. Shawn's dad."

Ben wanted to change the subject, but he knew Sam Brown was right, that Sam was just putting words to what they all knew was true. Ben more than anybody.

"I did think I could do something to get his attention. Coach's, I mean. I felt like every night, I made a couple of plays that *should* have gotten his attention. But he'd already made up his mind."

"Yeah," Sam said, "the day Shawn was born."

Lily pointed at Sam now.

"You *do* need to let this go," she said to him. "Because if you don't, Ben never will."

Turning and looking right at Ben now. Or right through him, sometimes it was hard to tell.

"You're the guy who's always telling me that size doesn't matter in sports," she said to Ben. "That when you're playing a game you always believe you're as big as anybody in it. I mean, you *are* still that guy, right?"

He nodded.

"So now you gotta be big enough to handle this. So you don't get to play quarterback this season. Boo hoo. Stop acting like somebody stole your bike."

Ben felt a smile coming on him that he couldn't have stopped if he tried. But then Lily had a way of making that happen. A lot.

"It kills me to admit this," he said, "but you're right."

"Duh," Lily said.

She turned to Sam. "Are we good on this?"

"No," he said. Just because he was Sam. "I might stop talking about him being the best QB we've got. But even you can't make me stop thinking it."

Sometimes Ben thought Sam was the only one of the three guys in the Core Four not afraid of Lily Wyatt.

"Fair enough," she said.

They heard Ben's mom calling from the other side of the street, wanting a head count on how many members of the Core Four would be staying for lunch today. Ben told her all of them.

Then he picked up the ball lying next to him, stood up, said to Sam, "Go long."

Sam did, flying toward the playground at the other end of the park, Ben letting the ball go and watching Sam run under it at full speed, catching it with his arms stretched out as far as they would go, finally having to dodge one of the swings at the last second like it was a tackler trying to bring him down in the open field.

Not a perfect spiral. Close enough.

This time Ben really had thrown it as far as he could.

"Now that's a stinkin' arm," Coop said, staring down the field to where Sam was standing with the ball.

"No, that was me doing what Lily told me to do," Ben said.

"Which is?"

"Letting it go."

Ben told his parents at dinner that night what Lily had said to him, told them he was through feeling sorry for himself, and that his new goal was to be the most valuable player on the team wherever Coach O'Brien wanted to line him up.

Beth McBain said, "It's probably silly of me to even mention this. But, um, haven't your dad and I been pretty much giving you the same advice? You're starting to make me question my ability as a salesperson."

Ben's mom had gotten her real estate license six months ago and gotten a job with a company in town, still managing to work out her schedule so that she was home every day by the time Ben got out of school. Jeff McBain ran the Rockwell YMCA.

"Maybe it's the same as when you've got two people trying to sell the same house," Ben's dad said, smiling at his wife. "Maybe Lily's presentation was just better."

She said, "This is such a witty family. Really, it's almost like living with the Simpsons."

"Mom," Ben said, "it's not that I don't hear you guys. But

you know that sometimes when stuff comes from one of your friends, it makes more sense to you. Or maybe I'm just plain old afraid to cross Lily."

"There is that," his dad said.

"So you're good now?" his mom said.

"Yep."

"Lily's a genius," Beth McBain said.

Ben groaned. "Please don't say that in front of her."

He knew he had said all the right things to his parents. And to Lily and Sam and Coop. And Ben had meant them.

But there was one more thing he had to do before he let go of his dream of being a quarterback for another season.

So he went upstairs to his room and closed the door and fired up his laptop and went to his Bookmarks and found the video of Doug Flutie making his throw one more time.

Ben only knew about Doug Flutie because his dad had played on the same team with Flutie at Boston College. So Ben knew that Flutie had won the Heisman Trophy his senior year, knew he was really only 5-9 even though they sometimes listed him as being taller.

Jeff McBain had graduated the same year as Flutie, which meant that he was on the field at the Orange Bowl the day the smallest guy on the field and one of the smallest to ever win a Heisman Trophy had thrown the most famous pass in college football history.

It was the day after Thanksgiving in 1984, Boston College against Miami on national television. Miami, which had won the national championship the year before, which had a star quarterback of its own in Bernie Kosar, had finally gone ahead 45–41 in the last minute of what had been a crazy game.

"You kept telling yourself all day that the last team with the ball was going to win," Ben's dad had said the first time he ever showed him the last few minutes of that game. "But then Bernie got them their last score and we had the ball on their forty-eight-yard line with just six seconds left, and I thought I was wrong. I thought Miami was going to win."

He had smiled then, at what Ben was about to see. "But Doug didn't."

By now, about to watch it again, Ben knew that the play was called "Flood Tip." From all the reading up on the game that Ben had done, he knew Doug Flutie wanted to hold on to the ball as long as he could, so that his receivers had a chance to get to the end zone.

Ben watched it now on his laptop screen. Watched Flutie drop back and scramble to his right.

This was from a show about the game and the throw that ESPN had done one time, and on the screen now Ben saw Flutie saying, "I got to the corner and let it rip."

He threw the ball more than sixty yards because he could, because even at 5-9 he had a huge arm. He threw it high and far down the middle of the field and unless you knew it was a completion, that the ball had ended up in the hands of Flutie's roommate and best bud Gerard Phelan — *Like I threw it to Sam*, Ben thought — you wouldn't have been sure right away that it was a completion. Even the announcers on the game that day weren't sure right away.

But it was a completion. Flutie had done the impossible. BC had won that game.

Ben watched him now, Flutie running and jumping down the field like he really was a little kid, then finally being lifted into the air by his teammates.

On the screen now, Bernie Kosar, who'd watched the play from his sideline the way Jeff McBain watched it from his, said, "The guy was a winner."

The screen went to black then. Ben thought about watching it again, he never got tired of watching it, watching the impossible become possible in front of his eyes. Watching a guy who'd become his favorite football player ever even though he'd never seen him play live. It was why he always wore No. 22 and asked for it again this season, because it had been Doug Flutie's number in college.

But Ben had decided that he wasn't going to watch the play again until the season was over. The play was about a quarterback, and he wasn't one, except in his own mind, and heart. For now, it hurt too much to watch Doug Flutie make the kind of play Ben dreamed about making someday on a football field.

It didn't just hurt. It made him mad. He knew Lily was right, that he had to let this go. But Sam was *more* right:

The best guys were supposed to play in sports. And Ben knew — in his mind, in his heart — that he was the best guy to play quarterback, no matter what the coach said, that he was the one who would give their team its best chance to win.

He closed his laptop.

Trying to convince himself there was more than one way to be a winner in football.

At the end of their first official practice for the Rockwell Rams on Monday night, Coach O'Brien came over to Ben and said they needed to have a talk.

The two of them walked to the back of the far end zone. When they got there, Coach said, "Step into my office."

Ben took off his helmet. "In the movies, this is when the coach tells the guy he's been cut."

"If I ever tried to cut you, the people who hired me would have to turn around and fire me," Coach O'Brien said. "You're too good. And I need you too much."

"Thanks."

He'd had a great first practice, two big runs out of the backfield, returning a punt for a touchdown at the very end when Coach had them work on special teams. Something else hadn't changed from last season to this one: Ben and Sam were still the two fastest guys on the team.

"Listen," Coach said, "I know you want to play quarterback."

Just coming right out with it.

Ben looked up at him. Way up. Matt O'Brien was 6-4. He knew because he'd checked it out on the Internet, just out of curiosity.

Ben waited.

"I saw how hard you went after it last week, how much you wanted it," Coach said. "I saw what kind of arm you've got on you. The only one here who's got a bigger arm is my own kid."

It sounded like one of those good news–bad news deals to Ben, so he just said "Thanks" again.

Coach said, "I didn't need a whole week to see you've got as much heart as you do talent for this game, despite your lack of size. I can see how tough you are, the way you get right back up no matter how hard you get knocked down. If you're tough enough to do that, you're tough enough to get straight talk from me, okay?"

"Okay."

"Shawn's a better quarterback than you are," he said.

Ben thought to himself: *Not like he's sugercoating it.*

Coach kept going. "He's not the player he's going to be someday, because someday he's going to be an even better player than I was. The things he's got, the size and the arm strength, you can't teach those things. And when he gets hot, man oh man, you can see how much potential he really has. I'm not just saying it's because he *is* bigger than you. I just believe he'll be able to help us more at his natural position. And you're going to help us everywhere else."

All Ben heard at the end was "*his* natural position." Like he'd been born with it.

Coach paused.

"It's important to me that you know this isn't just because he's my son," Coach O'Brien said. "That wouldn't be fair to him and it wouldn't be fair to anybody else. He's just a born quarterback."

Ben wasn't sure who he was trying to convince in that moment. Sometimes his parents were like this, analyzing things to death until you wanted to shout, *I get it!*

"Listen, I know he's wound up a little too tight on the field sometimes," Coach said. "I know sometimes he's trying *too* hard to make the perfect play or the perfect pass. But that's what great ones do. They put the most pressure on themselves. I always did."

Ben wasn't sure how he was supposed to respond to any of this. Or even if he was supposed to respond at all. So he just said, "Coach, you don't have to explain anything to me, I've got no complaints."

"I could call you a backup QB, but I don't want you to think of yourself as a backup *anything*," Coach said. "Because you're too valuable doing everything you're gonna do to help us win games."

The words came out of Ben's mouth before he could stop them. "But if you ever did have to put me in," he said, "you could. I know where everybody's supposed to be on every play."

He did.

He always did.

"Great," Coach O'Brien said.

To Ben, it felt as if he'd just been patted on the head.

Coach said, "Even last year, Shawn told me that having you is like having an assistant coach on the field. So, definitely, in an emergency, I could throw you out there. But one of my big things is that the leader of the team needs to be on the field. I saw that when I was backing up Peyton Manning in Indy. Guy never missed a down."

Ben nodded. Coach O'Brien got down on one knee now, put his hands on Ben's shoulders. "I need you to be great for me this season," he said. "I need you and Shawn needs you. He said that if I try to take you out of the game for more than a couple of plays at a time, *he'll* fire me."

"Like I said, Coach, I've got no complaints."

Coach stood up, groaning as he did, saying that once your knees go, they don't come back. Then he put out his hand. Ben shook it. Ben found himself wishing that he didn't like this coach.

But he did.

Coach O'Brien said, "Anything else you need from me?"

"Just the ball," Ben said.

It had been complicated between Ben and Shawn from the time they started playing together last season, even before Shawn's dad had started coaching the team.

There were no *huge* problems between them, even if Ben didn't always like the way Shawn acted on the field. There were other guys he wanted to tell to dial it down a notch once in a while when they got too excited after a good play or started acting crazy after a bad one. And there were other guys on the team who sometimes looked like blamers when something would go wrong. All part of being on a team. They all had the same goal — win the game — but they were all different.

Still: A year after Shawn had moved to town, Ben felt as if they really didn't know each other, almost like Shawn didn't care whether he got to know his teammates or not.

Shawn's dad wanted him to be a team leader, but as far as Ben could tell, he was anything but. Ben wanted him to be a leader, wanted him to act like a better teammate and a better guy. Wanted him to be the kind of player who made the other players better, because Ben thought that's what a quarterback should do.

He just wasn't sure how to do something about it. Or if it was his place to do something about it. If his own father couldn't get him to act like more of a team guy, how could one of his teammates?

And this was about more than Shawn having the job Ben wanted. At least Ben hoped it was.

Once the games started last season, they actually got along fine. Ben knew it wasn't like that with other guys on the team, but he never tried to big-time Ben, not once. In fact, over the last half of the season, when their team won five straight games and just missed going to the championship of the Bantam Division — the two teams with the best record getting to play for the championship — it was Shawn who went to Coach Bucci and told him Ben should be running the ball more and he, Shawn, should be throwing it less, now that his hot streaks were coming less and less frequently, when he was missing a lot more throws than he was making.

Shawn was still the one who got under center and called the signals. But when they got hot at the end of the year, made their run, he seemed happy to call Ben's signal as often as possible.

Suddenly being a better teammate than he had been all season.

In their last game, when they were coming from behind against Harlan, Shawn even did something he'd hardly done at all during the season, changed the play that Coach Bucci had sent in, calling for a short pass to Ben instead of a long one to Sam down the field.

"My call," he'd said to Ben at the time. "Your ball."

Coach didn't mind, as it turned out, Ben catching the ball in the backfield and running thirty yards to the end zone and Rockwell winning the game because he did. Afterward, he actually thought it was pretty cool, Shawn stepping out of the way when he could have looked like the star, pretty much tossing the ball and the game Ben's way. Fine with Ben. He *always* wanted the ball, in any sport he was playing. It was why he liked pitching and why he liked being a point guard.

Why he dreamed about being a QB someday. Someday and some*how.*

He wanted to be the one controlling the action in all ways, same as he did when he had the controls of a video game in his hand.

It was different with Shawn. Sometimes Ben thought that the real problem between Shawn and him, the thing keeping them from being friends, wasn't the position Shawn O'Brien played, it was that he just didn't seem to flat-out love football the way Ben did. That football was almost like an after-school job to him. It was one more thing about him that Ben didn't understand, almost made him angry sometimes, Shawn not seeming to appreciate having a job Ben wanted so badly.

It was why Ben finally decided to suck it up and somehow get to know Shawn better this season.

Before practice on Saturday morning, at the end of the second week, Ben told his mom he had to at least try to be friends with Shawn, mostly because it was the kind of thing you talked to your mom about.

She said, "Let me ask you this: What do the two of you usually talk about, when you *do* talk?"

"Football."

"*Just* football?"

"Pretty much."

Beth McBain laughed. "Men. I gave up asking your father, bless his heart, what he and the other guys in his foursome talked about when they played golf, because the answer was always the same."

Ben grinned. "Football?" he said.

"*Golf!*" she said.

"Boy," Ben said, "I didn't see that coming."

His mom said, "Listen, the only way for you to find out about this boy is to talk to him about something more than what you guys are playing on third down."

"What kind of play we're *running*, Mom. Not *playing*."

"You know what I mean," she said. "Talk to him. But *really* talk to him."

After practice, Ben did just that. Getting a minute alone with Shawn, asking him if he wanted to go get a slice of pizza in town.

"You and me?" Shawn said.

"Yeah. I figured we could go to Pinocchio's."

"Why?" Shawn said.

."Best slice in town?"

Shawn said, "You know what I mean."

Ben grinned and said, "I looked it up on my computer today. It's take a QB to lunch day."

Shawn didn't say anything back right away, Ben wondering if the guy had any sense of humor. Or just had no interest in being buds.

Until Shawn finally said, "Let me go ask my dad."

He ran over to where his dad was talking to one of the other parents, came jogging back with some money in his hand.

Shawn said, "He said he'd pick me up in an hour, and that I should pay."

"Cool," Ben said. "And *my* dad is always telling me that there's no such thing as a free lunch."

Shawn O'Brien never smiled much on a football field. But Ben noticed a small smile on his face now.

"Hold *on*," Shawn said. "You mean our dads *don't* know everything? Who knew?"

It was a short walk from Rockwell Middle School to the small downtown area in Rockwell. There were two pizza places in town, but the one Ben and his buddies like the best was called Pinocchio's, quiet by the time they got there, a little after two o'clock, only a couple of the booths filled.

Shawn asked what Ben liked and he said he usually got a half-pepperoni, half-plain.

"Same," Shawn said.

Something in common besides football.

A start, maybe.

While they waited Shawn said, "My dad was surprised when I told him you and I were gonna do something. He's always been asking me why we don't hang out more together."

"Same," Ben said.

Ben noticed that Shawn looked big even sitting across from him in their booth. You might not know he was a quarterback just looking at him, but you knew he was some kind of player.

"How do you think we're looking so far?" Shawn said. "The team, I mean."

They were going to start out speaking football to each other, maybe figure it out from there. Ben decided to go with it, just because for a change Shawn actually sounded like he was interested in other players on the team, not just himself.

"There's nothing we don't have," Ben said. "You, Sam. Enough big guys up front. Bunch of fast guys. My dad always says that two things you can't coach in sports are big and fast."

"And, we have you," Shawn said.

Ben let that one go, just adding, "Plus, we have your dad coaching us. That must be pretty cool for you guys."

"Oh, it's *awesome*," Shawn said, really stepping on the last word. "Dad tells people he's been waiting his whole life to teach a son of his how to be a quarterback. Said he was afraid after two daughters he was just going to keep having daughters and never get the chance."

"You guys are lucky," Ben said. "My dad is threatening to coach my Little League team next season. It would be the first time he's been my official coach. The last couple of years he's been totally busy because with the renovation at the Y it's practically like they're building a whole new one."

"Well," Shawn said, "my dad's got nothing *but* time for football now that he doesn't have a real job anymore. So he's *totally* focused on the team. And me."

"Yeah," Ben said, "I check him out sometimes and he's smiling his head off, watching every move you make."

"Tell me about it."

"He seems like such a good guy."

"*Great* guy," Shawn said. "But, dude, trust me, we better be great this season, because he's gonna take it *hard* if we're not."

"I'm not worried," Ben said.

"You never did last year, no matter how badly we were losing."

"My mom says the only word that's not in my vocabulary is 'can't,'" Ben said. "But I tell her, only if she stops with the *c*'s."

Their pizza was ready. They polished it off at record speed, hardly any talking now. When they finished, Shawn said, "My dad said he had a good talk with you."

"He didn't have to," Ben said. "He's the coach, I'm cool with whatever he wants me to do."

"Grown-ups love to have their talks," Shawn said, putting air quotes around "talks."

Before Ben could add anything to that, Shawn said, "He might not know how good you'd be at quarterback, but I do."

Ben didn't know why, but he felt Shawn had gotten down to it now, the real reason why he agreed to have lunch. Ben almost smiled. He wanted to get to know Shawn better, maybe even be boys with him, not thinking that Shawn might want to do the same with him.

But this wasn't a "talk" — with or without air quotes — that Ben wanted to have with Shawn. The one about how much he wanted to be a quarterback, how much he wanted what Shawn had and was probably going to have for a long time.

"Oh, don't stress on that," Ben said. "*My* dad tells me all the time that my real position is just football player. And everybody knows that you're a better QB than me."

Shawn started to say something, then stopped, like a pump fake on the field.

"That first night of tryouts? I saw that play you made after you scrambled. Aaron Rodgers doesn't throw on the run better than you do."

Everybody on the team knew how much of a Green Bay Packers fan Ben was. He had other teams he liked in sports. But even living a long way from Lambeau Field, the Packers were his favorite. And Rodgers was his favorite player now. He was a lot bigger than Doug Flutie. But Ben loved the way he played, especially every time he got flushed out of the pocket and had to improvise.

Ben drank some of his Gatorade and said, "Yeah, but I'm smart enough to know you can't do that on every down. Make stuff up as you go along, like it's some fun play I drew up in the dirt."

"You always seem to have fun," Shawn said.

"What, you don't?"

Shawn said, "Not like you."

"What's more fun than playing football?" Ben said.

"Oh, nothing," Shawn said. "Nothing at all. My dad is always saying that the worst day he ever had in pads was great."

"Pretty much my attitude," Ben said.

"Yeah," Shawn said. "You're lucky."

Shawn pointed to the big clock behind the counter. It was three o'clock. Shawn said his dad would be there any minute to pick them up. He paid the check and they went outside to wait, Ben thinking this had been a good idea.

A good day.

Except.

Except Ben couldn't shake the idea, like a defender he couldn't shake, that there had been something else Shawn wanted to talk about at lunch today.

That there was something Shawn had wanted to tell him, but hadn't.

Their first game was the next Saturday, home at The Rock against Midvale, which had made it to the championship game last season before losing to Darby.

Ben woke up early, the way he always did on game day, even earlier than he did when he had to go to school. Any game day always felt like some kind of holiday to him, but especially the first game of the season. So he was wide awake by seven o'clock, not needing an alarm, already feeling as if one o'clock, when the ball would be kicked off, would never come.

By eight o'clock Sam Brown was with him, having knocked on Ben's door and just walked in.

"Hey," he said.

"Hey."

Sam wasn't a big talker, even when Coop and Lily weren't around. Maybe it was one of the things that made the Core Four work as well as it did. Coop loved to talk, loved to make himself the center of attention, loved being the funny one, even though it chafed him to death knowing that Lily was actually much funnier, and without trying nearly as hard as Coop did.

So the two of them were always going at it, never in a mean way, like they were in some kind of competition that would last as long as they all were friends.

It was different when it was just Ben and Sam. Quieter. Sometimes the two of them could feel as if they were half-way into a conversation before either one of them had barely said a word.

"You ready?" Sam said.

"You know it."

Ben was already dressed, so Sam picked up the football sitting on top of the dresser, turned, and walked out with it, both of them knowing they were going across the street to McBain Field right now to start throwing it around a little bit, like this was the beginning of pregame warm-ups for Midvale, just the two of them.

They loosened up their arms and before long Sam was running some of the pass routes he'd be running against Midvale. Ben did the same. Then Sam, who also punted for their team, dropped back and kicked a few to Ben, who felt like an out-fielder getting ready for a game by shagging fly balls during batting practice.

When they finished, and were sitting in the grass, Sam said, "Okay, now I'm good."

"What's better than good?" Ben said.

"Your girlfriend showing up?" Sam said. Grinning the way he always did when he said that, casually pointing at Lily Wyatt riding her bike down the street.

"She's not my girlfriend," Ben said. "No matter how many times you call her my girlfriend just to get under my skin."

"Sorry," Sam said. "My bad. Don't know what I was thinking."

"She's *not* my girlfriend," Ben said.

"'Course not."

Lily leaned her bike against the maple tree and came walking over to them, smiling as if she had a game to play, too.

"Look at the two of you," she said.

"What?" Ben said.

"You look like it's Christmas morning and you're on your way to find out what's under the tree."

She was standing over them, hands on hips. Lily was taller than Ben, but not nearly as tall as Sam, both of whose parents were tall, and whose own pediatrician said might grow to be as tall as 6-4 someday. It's why as good as Sam Brown was in football, his favorite sport was basketball.

Ben wasn't sure what his favorite sport was, at least not yet. Usually it was just the one he was playing at the time, whatever was in season.

"Wow, that's pretty disrespectful comparing Christmas to football," Ben said, grinning at Sam, knowing Sam was way ahead of him. "Football's *way* more important than that."

Lily sighed.

"Sometimes," she said, "I think I should wait until after football season is over to have a normal conversation with you guys."

"For a girl . . ." Ben said.

"Here we go," Lily said.

". . . you can speak football pretty well," he said.

"For a girl," she said.

Ben said, "It's just that you're not always willing to try."

"Because I don't *care* enough to try," she said.

"You coming to the game?" Ben said.

"Wouldn't miss it," Lily said.

It felt like the whole Rockwell Rams team missed the game, at least the first half of it.

They were behind 12–0 and it could have been worse than that if Midvale's fullback didn't fumble on the Rams' five-yard line with thirty seconds left before halftime.

"Put it this way," Coop said to Ben as they walked off the field, "nobody would say we're exactly crushing it so far."

"We're gonna *get* crushed if we don't step on it a little," Ben said.

"You think I should give a halftime speech and remind the rest of the guys that, like, this isn't a scrimmage?" Coop said. "That the game *counts*?"

"I have a feeling the Coach is going to point that out without your help."

"That's what I'm afraid of," Coop said. "This is *not* going to be pretty."

Coach was fine, though, mostly telling everybody to relax, that not once in his whole career had he ever won a championship in the first half of the first game of the season. And had never lost one.

Coach O'Brien was actually smiling when he said, "We're down a couple of scores in a Pop Warner game. It's not like you're all going to be held back a year in school if we don't come back. Even though we *are* coming back."

He told them that he wasn't going to change much on his substitution pattern, not just because league rules said that everybody in uniform had to be out there for at least eight plays, but because he wanted to see what they all could do in a real game situation. Especially now that Midvale had come at them pretty hard.

"One of the greatest lines I ever heard in sports came from Mike Tyson, when he was still a great boxer and not in the movies," Coach said. "Before a fight one time he said, 'Everybody's got a plan till they get hit.' Well, we've been hit now. So we're the ones who are gonna have a different plan in the second half. Okay?"

They all nodded.

"But the plan does not include anybody on this team hanging his head," Coach said. "Got it?"

Hardly anything had gone right for them in the first half. Shawn had missed all but two of his passes. And the Shawn that Ben had started to like and wanted to like after the two of them shared a pizza together had gone right back to being the Bad Shawn he'd see at practice. Grabbing his helmet when he'd miss a pass, or somebody would drop one on him, as Darrelle had in the open field. Staring with his hands on his hips after Conor Hale, their left tackle, missed a block and Shawn got sacked.

But most of it was directed at himself today. One time, waiting for Kevin Nolti to bring in the play from the sidelines, Shawn walked a few yards away from the huddle, put his head down, and said to himself, "I *stink*!"

Not only was Shawn playing tight today, he was making the other guys on offense tight. The more he missed with his passes, the worse it got. And once Midvale realized the Rams had no real passing game, at least so far, they started bringing more guys up close to the line of scrimmage to stop the run, one of the big reasons why Ben's longest run from scrimmage had been four yards.

The one time he did slip out of the backfield to catch a short pass from Shawn — one of Shawn's two completions — Midvale's middle linebacker dropped him after a one-yard gain.

"You good?" Sam had asked Ben earlier in the day.

Not even close, Ben thought, *at least not so far.*

They had waited all summer for football season to start, even when they were having their summer fun playing All-Stars after the regular Little League season. Only now, even after a full half against Midvale, it was as if the season had somehow started without them.

When Mr. O'Brien finished talking to them, Ben went over to where Shawn was standing by himself behind the bench. Looking a little bit as if he *was* hanging his head despite what his dad had just told the team.

"We're coming back, dude, no worries," Ben said.

Shawn said, "I stink." At least he was consistent with that today.

"And that would be a problem if the game were over," Ben said. "Only it's not. We've got a whole half to play."

"I stink and we stink," Shawn said and walked away.

Coop came over and said to Ben, "How's the QB?"

"Sketchy," Ben said. "*Very* sketchy."

"Well," Coop Manley said, "at least he hides it well."

Out of nowhere, though, Shawn got hot at the start of the second half. Got on one of those streaks where he did show off his arm. They had run a couple of plays on their first drive, but got into a third and ten, and Shawn hit Justin for a first down. Then Sam for a short gain, then Darrelle, then Sam again over the middle. Even the Midvale players acted surprised, like, where was *this* guy in the first half?

Ben didn't try to figure out why Shawn had found his touch all of a sudden, and maybe a little confidence, mostly because he didn't care. All he cared about was that they were moving now. They were in the game.

Finally Shawn threw a short pass to Ben, who caught the ball in the right flat and didn't stop running until he was at the Midvale nine. Coach came right back to the play, and Ben was open again, but this time Shawn overthrew him. Badly.

Ben came back to the huddle and tried to make a joke out of it. "I'm too short for a lob pass," he said.

"I am a *total* loser today!" Shawn said.

Like all the passes he'd completed on the drive suddenly didn't matter, like all it took was one bad throw to stop believing.

"Dude, relax," Ben said. "We're still gonna score. Those guys on defense must feel like they're a car going in reverse."

Ben thinking that he'd added one more position to all the others Coach said he was going to play this season:

Cheerleader.

"Dude," Ben said, "it's just football."

"To you, maybe," Shawn said, and then told them the play his dad had just sent in from the sideline.

It was a draw play to Darrelle. Even though a defense usually has to be expecting a pass for a play like that to work best, Coop opened up a huge hole and Darrelle ran through it and the game was 12–6, where it stayed after Darrelle got stopped trying to run for the conversion. At this level of Pop Warner, hardly anybody was a placekicker yet, so teams always tried to either run or pass for two points.

But the Rams were on the board, that's what mattered. As they lined up for the kickoff, Ben said to Sam, "Our stupid alarm just didn't go off when it was supposed to."

Sam grinned. "Don't you just hate when that happens?"

It became a defensive game after that, neither team being able to move the ball, Midvale's Eagles still ahead by a touchdown until the last play of the third quarter, the Eagles punting from their forty-yard line. But their kicker, who didn't have nearly the leg that Sam did, hit this low, wobbly line drive that Ben read all the way, the way he did sinking line drives when he was playing the outfield. Got a great jump on the ball, caught it in perfect stride, already at full speed, just short of midfield.

He was halfway to the end zone from there before the guys trying to cover the punt for the Eagles realized how fast the play — and maybe the game — was going the other way.

The punter was the last guy with a chance as Ben angled toward the right sideline, the kid maybe thinking he had the angle on Ben now.

He didn't.

Because Ben cut back on him now, at full speed, saw the kid fall down when he realized he was being dusted that way. From there Ben could have run backward into the end zone with the score that made the game 12–12 at The Rock.

This time they tried to run a quarterback draw for the conversion. But Coop and Shawn messed up on the snap, the ball ending up on the ground between them. By the time Shawn picked it up, there was no chance for him to think about running the play as called. He nearly got to the outside, using his own great speed, going for the pylon at the front corner of the end zone. But one of the Eagles linebackers shoved him out of bounds before he could make it 14–12.

Coop was the first one over there, putting a hand out to help Shawn up, saying, "My fault, man."

Shawn ignored Coop's hand, just got up and walked past him, Coop's hand still hanging there in the air.

The way you did when you didn't want an opponent to help you up sometimes.

It didn't matter whose fault the bad snap was, not to Ben, anyway. All that mattered was that it was 12–12 and they still had a quarter left to play. The season really had started now. Big-time.

The Eagles got the ball back, made a couple of first downs. Had to punt. Same with the Rams. Two first downs, moved it into Eagles' territory. Sam had to punt.

There were three minutes to go when Midvale punted again, Ben having to make a fair catch because this time the kid had kicked the ball short and insanely high. Ball on the Rockwell forty-nine-yard line. All that green in front of them.

Tie game.

Ben looked over into the stands and saw Lily sitting with his parents. She smiled and pointed at him with both her index fingers. He quickly did the same, back at her, hoping nobody saw. Wanting to tell her she'd been right again, it really did feel like Christmas morning now.

As the rest of the offense came out on the field, Coach O'Brien came about ten yards out with them, telling them that Darrelle and Kevin Nolti, the other fullback, would be bringing in the plays. Telling them to run the plays like they did in practice. Telling them there was plenty of time to win the game.

"This is why anybody ever goes to the trouble of putting on all this equipment in the first place," Coach said.

He put his hand out. They put theirs in on top of it.

Coach said, "Do I even have to ask who wants it more?"

On the way out for first down, Coop said, "That was what Mrs. McCloskey would call a rhetorical question in English, you know."

Ben said, "Coop, no kidding, you're like half a genius."

"We might as well go ahead and win this sucker," Coop said. "Right?"

"Another rhetorical question," Ben said.

Coop said, "You think anybody else in town is having this much fun right now?"

"Not," Ben said, "if they're playing for Midvale."

Ben took a pitch from Shawn and ran eight yards before getting knocked out of bounds. Kevin ran for three. First down. Ben again, running right behind Coop this time for five. Then three more, off tackle.

The Eagles were still bigger. They could see that the Rams were running it on every down, whether they were in a pass formation or not.

But couldn't stop the Rams now. It was as if Coach wasn't going to start throwing again, or try to start throwing again, until the guys on Midvale's defense showed they could stop the run.

Coming back to the huddle after his second-down carry, Ben shot a look at Coach O'Brien, who looked like the calmest guy at The Rock, as if this was exactly where he wanted to be, too.

Or maybe, Ben thought, he just looked like somebody who had been here before.

Darrelle ran for the first down on third and two. The Rams at the Midvale twenty-five-yard line. Minute and a half to play. Coach decided to call one of the two time-outs he had left, motioning Shawn over to where he was standing on the sideline, then staring back at the clipboard with their plays on it.

When Shawn got back to the huddle, Ben said, "Any words of wisdom from your dad?"

"He told me he wants Darrelle to stay in for now," Shawn said. "So he gave me the four plays he wants us to run that he says are going to win the game."

"That's being pretty positive," Ben said.

"No," Shawn said. "That's just him being Dad."

This time Darrelle ran right up the middle behind Coop, for seven yards. They were inside the twenty now. Ben took another pitch from Shawn, running to his left this time, thought he might have enough of an opening to go all the way until their safety broke a block and shoved him out at the ten.

Minute left.

But then the Eagles' middle linebacker just planted Darrelle on first down, behind the line, almost hitting him before Shawn could hand him the ball. Two-yard loss. Shawn called the fourth play his dad had given him, handoff to Ben, with the option of taking it inside or outside their right tackle, Jack Wills. He took it outside. Again he thought he saw an opening. This time somebody tripped him up from behind, Ben going down at the Eagles' eight-yard line.

Third and goal.

Thirty seconds left.

Coach O'Brien called his last time-out.

Coach smiling at Shawn when he came over to him, putting both hands on his son's shoulders, obviously telling him the two plays he wanted Shawn to run, then leaning close to Shawn's face mask and saying one more thing before he sent him back out on the field.

"What did your dad say?" Ben said.

"He told me now I've got *two* plays to win the game," Shawn said. "But Dad says I'll only need the first one."

When Shawn called out "Sprint Left, Throw Back Right,"

Ben thought: *Love it.* Shawn was supposed to take the snap from Coop, roll to his left like he planned to run, stop, turn, throw it back across the field to Ben, who was supposed to be hanging around pretty much where he was when the ball had been snapped.

The play was always money in practice.

Better yet, it was a short, safe throw, and even though Ben knew he'd have downfield blocking if he needed it, Coach counted on Ben *not* needing it, counted on Ben's speed being all he needed to win the game.

"You get it to me," Ben said, "I'll get it in."

Then, one last time, Cheerleader Ben said to his quarter-back, "Relax and just let it happen."

Shawn ran hard to his left after taking the snap, selling the run like a champ. He knew he wasn't supposed to rush, that the defense had to bite, and didn't have to rush, because he had room and time.

At just the right moment, he stopped suddenly and threw.

Just not to Ben.

To the Midvale safety.

The fastest guy on *their* team.

Ben never saw the kid, No. 8, coming. Neither did Shawn, who'd just turned and thrown without checking the defense.

But somehow the safety read the play all the way. On TV, the announcers talked about defensive backs "jumping the route." That was what No. 8 on Midvale had done. Maybe he'd just guessed right. Or maybe he was smart enough to be spying Ben, saw Ben waiting for the ball.

"Players make plays," Ben's dad always liked to say when they'd be watching a game together and something great would happen.

The kid caught the ball in stride the way Ben had caught the punt he'd returned for a touchdown, already at top speed when he took the ball right out of Ben's hands. By the time Ben's brain had processed what had happened, the safety — as tall as Sam, as fast as Sam, which meant as fast as Ben — had at least a ten-yard lead on him.

Trying to take it to the house.

Another thing the announcers liked to say.

Ben McBain put his head down and ran as hard as he could, as hard as he had all day. As fast as he could. Feeling like he was starting to make up a little ground by the time the big kid from Midvale crossed midfield. Figuring Sam was probably chasing, too. But Sam had started even farther behind the play, in the end zone when Shawn threw the pick, right before the whole day had started going the wrong way.

Unless Ben could catch the No. 8 in red.

Knowing that if he didn't catch him, nobody on his team was going to, either.

Ben finally got as close as he was going to get just inside the Rams' ten-yard line, the kid with the ball having just looked over his shoulder to make sure nobody was gaining on him.

Now or never.

Ben launched himself, trying somehow to make himself

longer than he really was, got his hand on an ankle, just enough to knock him off balance.

Then watched from the ground as the kid stumbled and started to lose his balance, started to go down himself.

But not until he managed to fall across the goal line with the touchdown that made it 18–12 for Midvale.

The Rams got in one last play after Ben picked up the squibbed kickoff, managed to return it just past midfield.

Shawn took the snap and ran around and tried to throw it as far as he could to Sam Brown. But as strong as Shawn's arm was, even at eleven, he couldn't throw it nearly far enough. The ball ballooned on him a little bit and came down at the Midvale twenty-five. Sam managed to outjump the three defensive backs around him and come down with the ball. But got tackled right away, what looked like a mile from the end zone.

Sam was sitting on the ground with the ball still in his hands as the refs blew the whistle that meant the game was over and they'd lost.

It was usually one of the things Ben McBain loved about sports, how the very next thing that happened in a game — the game you were playing or the game you were watching — could be the one that changed everything.

But what he'd said to Lily turned out to be right: It wasn't nearly as much fun when it happened to you the way it had just happened in the Midvale game. Happened to you and happened to your team. When you were that close to being 1–0 and walked off the field 0–1 instead.

Coach had told them at halftime not to hang their heads. But it seemed as if they were all doing that now as they got into the line to shake hands with the Midvale Eagles. The day had changed to *great* for them at the very end, they were the ones who had seen a last-second loss turn into a last-second win.

Ben had looked around for Shawn after Sam caught his Hail Mary pass, but couldn't find him right away, maybe because the Midvale guys had run out to the middle of the field, celebrating as if they'd won a championship instead of just the first game of the year.

But Ben, even at his age, knew that sports could do that to you. Winning the game you'd just played, especially the way the Eagles had just won, *could* make you feel as if you'd just won the Super Bowl.

That's what they were feeling in the handshake line after the game.

While the line kept moving, Ben waiting to shake hands with the safety who'd scored the winning touchdown, tell him what a filthy play he'd made — "filthy" being the highest possible praise — Ben turned his head and finally spotted Shawn.

Only he wasn't behind him in the line, he was all the way on the other side of the field, alone on the Rockwell side, sitting at the end of the bench, head down, slapping his hands hard on the sides of his helmet.

It wasn't a rule that you had to shake hands with the players on the other team, win or lose. But Ben knew it was just something you did.

Ben could even see Coach O'Brien now up in front, congratulating the Midvale coach.

Finally it was Ben's turn to shake the safety's hand.

"Ben McBain," he said, introducing himself even though they'd just played a whole game against each other. "And hey? Let's do this again in the championship game."

"Brian DeBartolo," the other boy said. "And about the championship game? I'm totally down with that."

Ben knew he was holding things up, didn't care. "That play you made, it was, like, mad crazy," he said.

"Lucky guess," Brian said. "I just figured that when the game was on the line, they were going to you. And when your QB turned, he was *only* looking at you."

When he'd finished shaking everybody's hand, telling them good game, there was a moment, as Ben took the long walk back to the Rams' bench, when he tried to remember what he'd felt like in the morning. *Before.* But right now he couldn't, as hard as he tried. Truth was, he felt as bad as Shawn looked, still sitting there, same spot, end of the bench.

Even Coach O'Brien didn't go over there, as if he knew this was a time to leave his own son alone. Ben knew with his own parents: It was one of the things parents seemed to know. Not always. But sometimes they just seemed to know when there was a force field around you.

So he just motioned the rest of the guys to gather around

him in front of the bench, as if Shawn wasn't even a part of the team in that moment. Or maybe Coach just knew he could say whatever he wanted to say to Shawn later.

"Listen, guys," Coach said, "losing the first one this way will just make winning the first one next week even sweeter."

Then: "I'm not looking to give you a pep talk right now. Mostly because you don't want one. And I'm not gonna lie to you, it stinks having one get ripped away from us that way. But it's one game. Be proud of the way you fought back today, be proud of the way you took it down the field the way you did at the end. I knew we had talent with this group. Now I find out how much character you've all got. See you Monday at practice."

Ben wanted to go over and say something to Shawn, felt like he *ought* to say something. But before he had the chance, he watched Shawn stand up, take off his helmet, start walking by himself toward the parking lot.

And Ben knew what he wanted to say: That they won as a team and lost as a team, and not to be too hard on himself, they could all probably go back and find something, a play or two, that could have had them ahead before they tried to drive the ball down the field at the end.

Too late. Ben didn't want to make a show out of running to catch up with him. So he let him go, watched him take the long walk across the soccer field at The Rock and then the baseball field on the other side of that, to the parking lot where his dad's SUV was, Shawn getting smaller the farther away he got from the game he'd just played.

Looking to Ben in that moment as if he'd lost more than a football game.

The next thing Ben saw was Shawn's helmet flying through the air, bouncing high off the concrete in the parking lot, like *that* was his last bad pass of the game.

Ben couldn't stop thinking about how mad Shawn looked after the game. Like he was mad at the world. He thought about calling him Saturday night, just to see how he was doing, decided to leave it alone.

But after church on Sunday morning he told his mom that he was going to take a ride over to Shawn's house on his bike.

His mom said, "Don't you want to try calling him first?"

Ben said, "I'm afraid that if I do, he'll tell me not to come."

She smiled. "Like that would ever stop you."

"He makes it rough to like him sometimes. Really rough. But I just feel like I gotta do something, just to be a good teammate."

"Not 'good,' pal. Great. You're a great teammate."

They were both at the kitchen table, Ben having gotten out of his church clothes as though somebody had a clock on him, and having just polished off two bowls of cereal. His mom was cutting up fruit for the big fruit salad she made every Sunday to go with lunch.

She stopped for a moment, looked over at Ben. "I have to

say, though, sometimes I think sports is way too important to you boys."

Ben shook his head. "Sports are important, yeah, I hear you," he said. "But I don't think too important. You know how much I hate to lose, but it's not like I come home and you can't get me to come out of my room."

"That's just because no one would want to stay in that room for an extended period of time," she said, smiling at him. "The smell of the dirty socks alone . . ."

"Good one, Mom, no kidding, never heard *that* one before."

"Go on over there before you change your mind," she said. "And make sure you're back in time for lunch."

But when he got up he said to her, "Before I go, we need to do one more thing. So turn around."

"We just did this yesterday."

Ben said, "I'm feeling taller today."

Beth McBain turned around. So did her son. They got back-to-back and then Ben put his palm flat on top of his head and moved it back until he touched his mom's head. Measuring his height against hers.

"Getting closer," she said. "Definitely getting closer."

"Not close enough," he said.

"Go try to be Shawn's friend," she said. "You know what your old mom says about random acts of kindness."

"They turn us all into giants," Ben said, and then went to get his bike out of the garage.

• • •

Ben had never been to Shawn's house, but he knew where it was, a few blocks from where Coop lived at the north end of Rockwell.

Coop had seen the house, said he and his dad had walked over there to check it out one night after the O'Briens had moved in, having heard how big the place was.

"My dad," Coop had said, "said he wanted to go inside sometime just to see where the gift shop is."

And every kid in school had heard about the fifty-yard turf field at the back of the property, with goalposts and yard lines and, according to Shawn's buds who had seen the field, even an electronic scoreboard.

But as big as Coop said Shawn's house was, it was even bigger to Ben's eyes. If there was anything bigger than this in the whole town of Rockwell, Ben sure hadn't ever seen it. There was a gate near the road, where you had to be buzzed in, and what looked like a driveway that stretched nearly all the way to Darby.

Way up in the distance, Ben could see Mr. O'Brien's black SUV parked near the front doors.

Ben knew that Shawn had two older sisters, one of them just a year older, so there were at least five of them living here. *Yeah*, Ben thought, *and with enough extra room to maybe house our whole team.*

He pressed the button on the intercom, finally heard Mr. O'Brien say, "Who is it?"

Ben gave his name, said he was here to see Shawn.

The gates opened.

Ben tried riding up the gravel driveway, gave up about half-way, walked his bike the rest of the way from there. When he got close he could see Coach O'Brien — he thought of him as his coach, even here — waving at him from the porch.

"There's a part of the Boston Marathon called Heartbreak Hill," he said to Ben. "That's what Shawn calls this driveway." He smiled. "Of course that was when my boy was still communicating with the rest of the human race."

Ben said, "I didn't get a chance to talk to him after the game. I was gonna run after him, but he didn't look like he wanted any company."

Ben didn't say anything about Shawn throwing his helmet. As soon as Shawn had yesterday, Ben turned around to see if his dad had seen, but Mr. O'Brien was talking to the Midvale coach.

"I know you've got good moves on the field," Coach said, "but that might have been your best one of the day." He shook his head. "Guys I played with in the pros didn't take losing that hard. It's like by the end he couldn't remember all those passes he completed to start the second half."

"We all played well in the second half," Ben said, "except for one play."

"I tried to tell Shawn that the guy I played behind, Peyton Manning himself, once threw an interception like that against the Saints that cost my old team a Super Bowl."

"I just want to let Shawn know that we need him to get to where we want to go," Ben said.

"Have at it," Coach said, showing him in. "Maybe he'll

listen to you, because he's completely tuned me out for the time being."

"Is he in his room?"

"Down on the field. C'mon, I'll take you back there, it's pretty cool."

Shawn's dad took Ben through the house and out the back door and across a lawn that was about twice the size of McBain Field and then down a hill. And as soon as he saw the field, Ben knew that "cool" didn't come close to describing it.

Cool was playing the new Madden video game every season, or getting to stay up late to watch a game on television even on a school night.

But the field behind Shawn O'Brien's house was one of Coop Manley's favorite expressions:

Off the hook.

It *was* a turf field, looking brand spanking new, with lines that looked like they'd just been painted with the brightest white paint possible. There were goalposts, and the end zone had the Colts' logo on it, the same horseshoe you saw on their helmets.

"Wow," Ben said.

Coach said, "I've heard about guys who built their own basketball courts, sometimes even inside their homes. And golf nuts who built their own putting greens, or even a few holes if they had the room. But I'm a football guy. When I built my dream house I decided to build my dream backyard, too, for me and my boy."

"Wow," Ben said again, like he was stuck.

"Sometimes," his coach said, "I pretend I'm the eleven-year-old and sneak down and use that thing myself."

"That thing" was a remote-controlled pass receiver, like a little robot on wheels, moving from side to side across the field. Like a golf cart with a net on top instead of a roof. Shawn had a bunch of balls at his feet, and Ben could see the remote on the ground in front of him, too.

When he was ready, he pointed the remote at the robot, took a snap from an imaginary center, dropped back, and tried to lead the machine just right as it moved across the field, and deliver the ball into the net.

He just missed the net, maybe by a foot, shook his head, pointed the remote to stop the machine. Got another ball. Pointed again. Threw a strike into the net this time.

"If you're a quarterback," Coach O'Brien said, "you've got to be able to hit what you aim at."

"That was a good-looking throw."

Shawn's dad said in a quiet voice, "My kid got reminded yesterday that it's a little harder when you've got a bunch of big guys running at you. But he'll figure it out."

In a much louder voice now he called out to Shawn, saying, "Hey, pal. Somebody here to see you."

Shawn looked over, gave Ben a wave, then put up a finger that meant one more. Pointed the remote again, took a three-step drop, waited until the machine was in the middle of the field — he must have been able to speed the thing up, because it seemed to be moving faster this time — and buried another perfect strike into the net.

Ben went down and joined him on the field, the fake grass feeling even better than real grass under the Reeboks he had on, the ones with the Packers logo on the sides.

Ben said, "Lookin' good."

"Easy when you're by yourself."

"Easy for everybody."

"I didn't know you even knew where I lived," Shawn said.

"I think people in foreign countries know about this house," Ben said. He grinned and said, "Needed to see the field, and couldn't wait anymore for you to invite me. You must have guys here all the time."

Shawn said, "Mostly me and my dad."

Then: "Please tell me you really aren't here to tell me to keep my head up, or whatever."

"Nah," Ben said, still grinning, "I figure I've got my whole life to start sounding like my parents."

"So no talking about the game?"

"Not unless you want to," Ben said. Reached down and picked up a ball and flipped it to Shawn. "Let's just throw it around a little. But I'm warning you: I'm a lot trickier than Chad Ochocinco on Wheels."

"The thing I like best about him," Shawn said, nodding at the robot receiver, "is that he doesn't talk. Or tell me how to get better."

Ben took off down the field, feeling even faster on turf, made a sharp cut. Shawn hit him in the hands with a perfect spiral.

"Let me warm up *my* arm before I send you out," Ben said, and so the two of them soft-tossed for a few minutes before Ben's arm was loose.

And then for the next half hour or so they both turned it loose, long throws and short ones, buttonhooks and post patterns and fly patterns down the sideline, sometimes dropping back to throw, sometimes throwing on the run, both of them making the occasional diving catch.

"You really don't have guys lining up to come over here?" Ben said.

"Like I said, mostly Dad and me. He calls this my classroom."

Ben said, "Listen, if this is a classroom, I want to sign up for the course right now."

"Then you could be his prize pupil," Shawn said.

They went for a few more minutes. But even here, Ben could see Shawn straining to make every throw perfect, see him talking to himself up the field when he'd miss, one time yelling, *"Idiot!"* when he led Ben too much on a crossing pattern.

It was the same as in the game: No matter how many good throws he'd make, a bad one would make him lose his mind.

Finally they finished, at least for now, both of them out of breath and sweating. Shawn asked Ben if he wanted a drink and Ben said he was fine, Shawn didn't have to go up to the house. But Shawn said he didn't have to go up to the house, walked over behind the bench — underneath the small electronic scoreboard — and took two Gatorades out of a fridge Ben hadn't even noticed at first.

Ben took a swig and said, "The only thing missing, maybe over on the other side of the field, is one of those giant TV screens like they have in real stadiums."

"Don't give my dad any ideas."

"It must be amazing, having a dad who played QB in the pros."

"Yeah," Shawn said. "You have no idea."

Shawn stretched out on the bench, Ben on the turf, hands behind heads, staring up into the blue sky, and talked football. Just not Pop Warner football. Not Rockwell vs. Midvale. Shawn wanted to know why Ben ended up a Packers fan and Ben told him he started rooting for Aaron Rodgers after Brett Favre left the Packers, how he felt like Rodgers was an underdog having to follow Favre in Green Bay, and he'd always rooted for underdogs, maybe because he was small.

"But Rodgers isn't small," Shawn said.

"Maybe he just seemed smaller when he was starting out, because Favre had been so big for so long," Ben said.

Shawn said, "I watched all his interviews after the Packers won the Super Bowl last year. The guy always believed that things were gonna work out for him, that he was gonna justify the faith the Packers had in him. And I thought, What's up with *that*? The guy had nothing to go on when he first got the job."

"You gotta believe in yourself in sports," Ben said.

"That's what my dad tells me, all the time."

"Oh, come on, you gotta know how good your arm is," Ben said.

"What I know is, there's more to being a QB than just having an arm. Or making a few throws."

Ben rolled over so he was propping himself up on an elbow, looking at Shawn now. "I sort of did come over to talk about the game."

"Shocker," Shawn said.

Ben had thought about what he wanted to say to him the whole way over, like it was a talk he had to give in front of the class without any notes.

He took a deep breath.

"Listen," he said. "My dad said something to me one time I never forgot. We were watching one of the pregame shows and some player said it was a 'must-win' game for his team. And my dad goes, 'Okay, but what if you *don't* win?'"

Shawn was sitting up now, long legs crossed in front of him on the bench, his face serious, doing what Ben had asked him to do. Listening.

Whether he was hearing or not was another story.

Ben kept going.

"When you're the quarterback," Ben said, "everybody's looking at you. *Because* you're the quarterback."

"And the coach's son," Shawn said. "Don't forget that part." He smiled but Ben didn't think he meant it. "I *never* forget."

"You just gotta forget everything and play."

"Easy for you to say," Shawn said.

"We all want to win," Ben said. "You just can't let losing eat you up like it did yesterday."

Ben saw Shawn's face start to redden, like he'd just missed with another pass, heard him say, "You don't know me."

"Trying, dude. Trying."

Ben wished he had Lily with him, she always knew how to say the right things, even when she was busting on him, or Sam, or Coop. Plus, she had more common sense than any other kid he knew. But she wasn't here, so Ben did the next best thing, tried to get her voice inside his own head, trying to find the right words.

"I'm not saying you're supposed to *like* losing, especially like that," Ben said. "You just can't let it show the way you did yesterday. I'm telling you as a friend."

Shawn gave him a long look and said, "Thanks."

"Just thought you needed to hear that."

"No," Shawn said. "The part about us being friends."

Ben grinned. "It is what it is."

Shawn said, "You sure my dad didn't put you up to this?"

"Nah, I'm just a dope trying to get you to chill a little."

"You're not," Shawn said. "A dope, I mean. I know I'm the one who acts like one sometimes. I just can't help myself, I guess."

Then he said, "I couldn't help it after the game. I let everybody down."

Ben said, "Seriously? So what? You were trying to make a play. Trying to win us the game. Maybe if I'd been paying closer attention, I could have come to the ball better."

"Stop," Shawn said, his voice louder than it had been. "Making excuses, I mean. My dad does enough of that for me."

Man, Ben thought, this guy *was* rough. Today he didn't want you making excuses for him. The day before, he blew off Coop because of a bad snap that was as much his fault as Coop's.

Ben could see Shawn's face getting red again.

"I get scared in games," Shawn said. "I want to do well so badly, as much for my dad as for me, that I try *too* hard. And then as soon as something goes wrong . . ."

He put his hands out, like he was helpless to explain it to Ben any better than that.

Just the two of them out here behind the house. But really trying to be friends now. Be *boys*. Doing what you did at their age, trying to understand stuff.

Ben said, "So you get scared sometimes. It happens."

"*All* the time."

"*No*, it doesn't. If it did, you'd be throwing picks or fumbling snaps on every play."

Shawn was the one taking a deep breath now, the air then coming out of him in a big blast, saying, "The bigger the play the smaller *I* play. Maybe you didn't notice as much last year, because we won all those games at the end. But believe me, I noticed."

"Everybody gets scared out there," Ben said. "Even pros get scared. I read one time that this guy Bill Russell, played for the Celtics about a hundred years ago, used to boot before every single game."

Shawn tried to smile. "Whoa, I'm not that bad. I'm not booting."

"You're not bad at all!" Ben said. "You gotta find a way to have fun. This is *supposed* to be fun."

"You're not listening. It's not fun for me."

Ben looked at him, this kid who seemed to have it all.

"So we gotta figure out a way to make it fun," Ben said.

If Shawn heard, he didn't let on, just got up off the bench and came over to where Ben was sitting.

"You said we were friends now, right?" he said.

Ben grinned, stretched out his arms, like it was the most obvious thing in the world. "Well, *yeah*."

"I'm not so good at being friends with guys. But when somebody is your friend, you can trust the guy, right?"

"Right," Ben said.

"So if I tell you something and you swear you won't tell anybody else, you won't. Right?"

"Swear," Ben said. "Like they say in the movies, I don't talk even if I'm caught behind enemy lines."

But Shawn wasn't kidding and Ben could see he wasn't kidding.

"Swear on your heart?"

Ben went along, kept his own voice serious, put his hand over his heart and said, "On my heart."

"I don't want to play quarterback," Shawn O'Brien said.

Ben said, "Come on, man, you made one lousy pass."

"No, you don't understand," Shawn O'Brien said. "I *never* wanted to play quarterback in the first place."

Ben stared at him, hoping he didn't look as surprised as he felt. Knowing he'd heard right, but not quite believing. Shawn had *never* wanted to play quarterback.

Really?

"You ever tell your dad that?" Ben said.

What came out of Shawn O'Brien now wasn't much more than a whisper.

"I can't," he said.

"You *can't?*"

"My dad always says this is his dream backyard," Shawn said. "He tells everybody that. But his real dream is *me*. Not just me being a quarterback. Me being even a better quarterback than he was. It's the most important thing in the world to him. No, no way I can tell him this. *Ever.*"

Ben McBain liked to think he was pretty good, at least in sports, at anticipating what was going to happen next.

Not this time.

"That's why you have to help me," Shawn said.

"Help you with what?" Ben said.

Completely lost.

Shawn said, "You have to help me be a quarterback."

Not fair.

That was Ben's first reaction once he was back on his bike. First reaction and second and third as he took the long way home, going through town, giving himself some time to cool down, trying to figure out what had just happened.

But as fast as his bike was, it couldn't outrun this:

How totally unfair it was for him to be in this situation.

Forget about the guy not loving football the way Ben did. Forget *that*. Forget that he didn't love having a job that Ben would have given anything to have.

A job, by the way, he practically got handed with a bow around it.

Oh no, it was much better than that, he didn't even *want* the job.

Sweet.

Ben McBain couldn't remember a time 'when he *hadn't* wanted to play quarterback.

And even *that* wasn't even the craziest part. The really mad crazy part was that for Ben to be something that was even more important to him than being a quarterback — being a good teammate — now he had to be Shawn O'Brien's quarterback coach.

Forget about what Sam might do if he found out Shawn's "secret." Ben wanted to tackle the guy, too, even though he knew better, knew that wasn't him, that he had to help the guy even though Shawn had put him in a bad spot by swearing him to secrecy.

Talk about taking one for the team.

Check it out: Ben couldn't tell his parents what he knew about Shawn. Couldn't tell Sam or Coop. Couldn't tell Lily. She was the one worrying him the most. Trying to keep something from her was going to make Science seem like fun in comparison. Ben knew he was going to have to be careful around her, because if he wasn't, Lily would get that radar of hers going and demand to know what was up. Then he'd be in an even *worse* spot than he already was, because he and Lily had made their own pact all the way back in third grade, Lily making him swear that he'd never keep any secrets from her.

Ever.

And never lie to her.

Ben had never been much of a liar, anyway, lying had always seemed way too hard, no matter *how* hard telling the truth about something might seem.

The real truth right now was that he wished he'd never gone over to Shawn's, that he'd stayed home and played video games. Or read a book.

Sometimes when he was reading a book — Ben McBain loved reading almost as much as he did sports — he'd write down a sentence or two he wanted to remember. One time, he couldn't remember the book right now, he'd written down this quote, just because it had struck him funny:

"No good deed goes unpunished."

When he'd shown it to his mom she'd smiled at him and said, "You gotta be prepared for something, pal. No matter how much you think you're doing the right thing, life can still take a wrong turn on you."

Like now.

Before Ben had left he'd said to Shawn, straight up, "So, like, you're going to keep playing quarterback even though you don't want to?"

"I just have to get through this season," Shawn had said. "Then maybe I'll figure it out after. I keep hoping that Dad won't want to coach *next* season, that it's not his plan to coach me every year until I get to high school."

Ben had said, "So you're doing this for him?"

"I can't let him down," Shawn had said, almost whispering even though it was just the two of them. "And maybe if I got a little better I'd be a little less afraid."

·They had been walking back up the hill by then.

"Afraid of what?"

"Of letting everybody down."

"And you think I can help you?"

"You have to," Shawn had said.

As he started up his block, Ben was thinking maybe

he was the one who ought to be afraid, that maybe he'd finally promised something he wasn't going to be able to deliver.

Yeah, he thought.

Definitely should have stayed home today.

Ben had never thought there were certain things he had to *do* to be a quarterback, like some kind of to-do list, even in pickup games. Once the pickup games started, he just *was* a QB. Just let it happen. If the play broke down, he made up another one on the fly. He'd seen this one play on YouTube, another Flutie play, where Flutie got jammed up in the backfield and the only way for him to complete a pass was throwing the ball behind his back, the way you would in basketball.

Make it up, if you had to.

Just make the play.

Shawn was different. Oh man. No matter what the situation against Midvale, no matter what happened after the ball was snapped, Shawn had only changed the play his dad had sent in as some kind of last resort. Coach O'Brien could talk all he wanted in practice about secondary receivers. Shawn would still get locked in on the guy who was supposed to be getting the ball. The way he'd locked in on Ben right before the interception the day before.

It was almost as if Shawn was the robot like the one in his backyard, maybe thinking his dad was controlling him with a remote from the sideline.

It was almost time for the McBain family's Sunday lunch when he got back, the big bowl of fruit salad already on the dining room table. Sam and Coop and Lily were coming over to hang out later, after the Packers played the one o'clock game on TV, which meant Ben had some time before he had to explain to them why the Core Four might be about to become five for a while.

He'd gotten Shawn to agree to this: Ben could tell Sam and Coop that they were going to do some extra workouts on their own. So that they could all become more comfortable with one another. It was a legit idea, especially for Shawn and Coop, because they *had* messed up that handoff against Midvale, and it didn't matter whose fault it was, the ball still ended up bouncing around on the ground.

And it was *totally* legit that Shawn getting extra practice throwing to Sam could only help, since Sam was clearly the best receiver on the team.

Ben and Shawn agreed that the workouts would take place at McBain Field, even though Shawn's field was a whole lot better, both Ben and Shawn agreeing that Shawn would be a lot more relaxed without his dad being some kind of eye in the sky at the top of the hill.

Wanting to come down and help out.

"I mean this in a good way," Shawn O'Brien had said, "but my dad is already helping enough."

Ben was on his bed now, stretched out on top of the covers, hands behind his head, staring at the ceiling. Thinking: It wasn't just the game you were playing or the one you were watching that could turn around in a blink, sometimes it was your life.

He had come into the season wanting one thing: To be a quarterback. When he saw that wasn't going to happen, he just wanted things to be a little less complicated between him and Shawn, and now look where he was.

He heard a small knock on the door, said "Enter," saw his dad's smiling face appear from behind the door. Never a bad thing.

"'Bout five minutes until lunch," he said.

"You need help setting the table?" Ben said.

His dad tilted his head to the side, frowning, trying to look confused. "Well, the boy definitely *looks* like Ben McBain," his dad said. "And he *sounds* like Ben McBain. But if he's talking about laying out forks and knives, he can't possibly *be* Ben McBain."

"No kidding," Ben said, "sometimes you and mom really are funnier than TV parents."

"Well," his dad said, "you're nice to notice." Then: "How'd it go at Shawn's? Your mom told me you were heading over."

"It went okay, I guess."

"Just okay?"

He wanted to tell his dad all of it, tell him how maybe the only way to save the season was to help Shawn get better — and get more confidence — playing a position he didn't even want to play. Ben wanted to ask his dad for advice, *totally*. But knew he couldn't.

All he said was "He's one of those guys who just wants it so bad it makes him *play* bad."

No lie there.

Then Ben added, "Dad, does that make *any* sense?"

"Actually," Jeff McBain said, "it makes perfect sense." His dad smiled at him again, the kind that could feel like a hug even from across the room. "It's the kind of thing that happens to parents all the time when they become too parental. Sometimes we want to be great parents so much we end up acting like idiots, and if you tell your mom I said that, no dessert."

"What is dessert, by the way? She wouldn't tell me."

"Banana cream pie."

"I won't talk." Ben sat up. "Dad, I *gotta* find a way to prop him up. I'm just not sure I know what's the *best* way."

The whole truth there, nothing but.

"Maybe you can convince him that he can help the team more by wanting it a little less," Ben's dad said. "Does *that* makes sense to *you?*"

Ben nodded, smiling back at him, because it did.

"Mom says Lily's the genius," he said. "Actually it's you."

"Now *that* you can tell your mother," his dad said.

He wasn't going to lie to his buds, he was just going to leave some stuff out, basically. He didn't think Shawn's secret — about not wanting to play quarterback — should be that big a secret. But it was. Because it was Shawn's secret.

And Ben had promised.

His mom would tell him sometimes when she was going over one of his English papers, it wasn't what you put that made your writing better, it was what you left out.

And Coop talked all the time about what he called the "Bro Code," what guys were allowed to do and say and what they weren't, Ben and Sam just rolling their eyes when he did, knowing he was just making up rules as he went along.

One time Ben pressed Coop on what he thought was the single most important part of the Bro Code and Coop thought about that for a minute and said, "Having each other's backs, no matter what."

Sam and Coop both knew Ben would have their backs, no matter what the situation. But this situation was different: For now, Ben had to have Shawn's back, too. He was already hoping that when Shawn started to see how much he could trust the Core Four, he'd tell the others that he was only playing quarterback to please his dad.

Ben knew that no matter how much he could justify what he was doing, he and Sam and Coop had always told one another everything. If they got their feelings hurt later because Ben had been holding back on them, Ben would have to deal with that. Maybe that was the *real* Bro Code.

For now, though, he needed to keep it simple: Shawn was too tight, they had to find a way to loosen him up.

When he explained that to Sam and Coop in his basement, Coop said, "And this is our job . . . why?"

They had decided not to watch a movie after the Packers game, had been playing Madden on the big screen instead. When Lily found out there was no movie, she called and informed them her idea of fun wasn't watching them lose their minds over a video game, but she *might* wander by later if there was time before supper.

"It's not our *job*," Ben said. "He's our teammate, and he asked for our help. So it's like when you help a teammate up after he gets knocked down in a game."

He looked over at Sam, down at the other end of the long couch. Waiting for some backup. Only this time it wasn't coming.

"Count me out," he said.

"You're kidding, right?"

Sam said, "You're the one that must be kidding. If I'm gonna do some extra work, it's not gonna be with him. Or *for* him."

"Same," Coop said. "It might be your idea of the Code to prop this guy up. Not mine. You heard the way he called me out yesterday?"

"Everybody says stuff they don't mean," Ben said. "You've done it plenty of times."

"Dude," Coop said. "Trust me. He meant it."

"The only guy on the team who doesn't think Shawn is a jerk is you," Sam said.

"He's not that bad," Ben said.

"You say," Coop said.

"You're really not gonna do this?" Ben said.

Feeling himself starting to get hot.

"I'd do almost anything for you and you know I would, because I have," Coop said. "But I don't feel like playing today. And I really don't feel like playing with *him*."

"I'd do it for you guys," Ben said, "if you asked."

Sam said, "I wouldn't ask."

Ben knew he had to drop it. They never fought. And he didn't want to fight over Shawn O'Brien. And could feel them getting close.

Or maybe they were already there.

"The guy's a teammate, that's all I'm saying," Ben said.

Like he was back to talking himself into something, convincing himself he was doing the right thing, as hard as it was.

Sam and Coop were at the bottom of the stairs now, on their way out. Sam looked at Ben and said, "He's our team- mate? Maybe you could tell him to start acting like one."

Ben waited a few minutes and then went upstairs himself. He still needed one more player to give Shawn the kind of workout he planned, and he knew where to find one.

Ben was throwing the ball around with his dad when Shawn showed up on his bike. When Ben had told Jeff McBain what he had planned for Shawn, his dad had said, "Love it."

"You don't mind?"

"I tell you all the time," his dad said. "I can still run straight ahead. I just can't go backward anymore."

Without telling his dad more than he should, without breaking his promise, Ben said, "I think he could use a little break from his dad, but he didn't say anything about mine."

Ben told Shawn it was a simple drill. His dad would rush him as hard as he could. Shawn had to get his pass off to Ben before getting touched. But instead of the three count or five count you usually gave the quarterback in touch football, Ben said Shawn wasn't getting any count.

"Instead of one-Mississippi, two-Mississippi," Ben said, "I'm sort of giving you *no*-Mississippi."

"I'm not feelin' you on this," Shawn said.

"My dad's bigger than anybody who's going to rush you," Ben said. "And he's gonna give you less time than you'd get in a game even if there was this almost perfect-o blitz. And you're gonna find out if you can still stand in there and complete passes."

"I tell Ben all the time," Ben's dad said, "that part of the fun of sports is finding out you can do things you didn't know you could."

Ben said, "It'll be fun."

"Maybe for you."

Ben said, "Nah. For both of us. You don't need to make perfect throws every time. But I'll bet you make more than you thought you would."

Ben's dad didn't rush Shawn as hard as he could, but did come at him pretty hard, even yelling his head off sometimes as he did. At first Shawn tried to get rid of the ball too quickly, missing Ben on short patterns, the ball flying all over the place almost like he was throwing it away on purpose.

"See what I mean," Shawn said to Ben. "I even stink here."

Ben could see him working as hard as he could to control his temper. Not for Ben's benefit. For Ben's dad.

Ben said, "Relax, dude. You'll get better at it."

Ben wasn't sure he believed that. But thought it sounded good.

Slowly, though, Shawn *did* get better over the hour the three of them were out there. He wasn't Ben Roethlisberger standing in against the rush until the last possible moment. Or Rodgers or Mike Vick throwing accurately on the run. But he started connecting on his passes. Ben's dad would end the play by getting a hand on him once in a while. Just not as often the longer they stayed at it.

Ben had already called "last play" a couple of times, wanting Shawn to end with a good throw, like they were shooting hoops and Ben wanted to make sure Shawn made his last shot.

But Shawn had underthrown Ben on one pass, then threw the next one wide and outside.

"Okay," Ben said. "*Last* last one, and this time I mean it."

"Good," his dad said. "Because now I can't even run straight ahead."

Finally Shawn delivered the goods. It looked like Ben's dad was on him, but then Shawn pump-faked, got Ben's dad to go flying past him, scrambled to his right, motioning with his left hand for Ben to go deep, planting and throwing and delivering a perfect strike at least thirty yards down McBain Field.

Money.

Money, money, money, Ben thought.

Ben reacted as if they'd gotten a do-over on the end of the Midvale game, sprinting back and jumping in the air and giving Shawn a flying chest bump, nearly falling down in the process.

"Okay," Ben said, "now *that* sucker we can quit on."

Ben's dad said, "Throw like that against Hewitt on Saturday and we'll be just fine."

"I'll try," Shawn said.

"See, that's the thing," Ben said. "*Don't* try. Just let it happen."

Shawn smiled and said, "Okay, I'll try *that.*"

"You'll be fine," Ben's dad said to him. "And now I am going to go across the street and spend the next several years in a hot bath."

Just Ben and Shawn on the field now. Shawn reached out with his fist and Ben tapped it. He didn't know if this was real or not, if this was the real Shawn, the way he wasn't sure if the Shawn he'd been with at the O'Briens' field was real.

But he'd go with this one for now. And found himself wishing that Sam and Coop *had* stuck around.

"Thanks," Shawn said.

"What friends are for," Ben said.

Shawn got on his bike and left. When he was out of sight down the street, Lily Wyatt stepped out from behind the maple tree and said, "Hey, you."

"Hey, yourself," Ben said, surprised to see her. "How long have you been here?"

"Long enough."

"You've been spying?"

"Observing," she said. "*Huge* difference."

She raised an eyebrow on him, the way she did sometimes, knowing she was good at it. When Ben tried to practice the same look in a mirror, he just looked confused.

"What?" he said.

"Nothing," Lily said.

"You're giving me a look."

"What look?"

"You know what look."

"I have no idea what you're talking about," Lily Wyatt said. "But I will make one observation, off my observing."

Ben waited.

Lily said, "Nobody gets that happy in a pretend game."

"The guy made a great throw."

"Even I could see that," Lily said. "But you acted as if your new friend had just won the championship of the entire universe."

"Well, maybe we did get a little too excited," Ben said. "We're just trying to prop him up on account of the way yesterday's game ended."

He saw her staring at him now. Giving Ben what he thought of as her "big eyes." When she did that, Ben usually found himself wanting to hide his own thoughts.

"Anything you're not telling me?" Lily said.

Ben and Shawn were able to work out a couple of more times at McBain, after school on Tuesday and Friday. Just the two of them. Both times Ben asked Sam and Coop to join them.

Both times Sam and Coop said no.

Ben asked them why they were so dug in on Shawn, and Coop said, "I don't have to know who I don't want to know."

"But you really *don't* know him."

"Well, then, problem solved," Coop said.

"What about you?" Ben said to Sam.

Sam said, "I'm waiting to see if he'll be as good a friend to you as you are to him."

Then Sam said, "It's hard enough acting like I'm happy to be catching passes from him — when he gets one anywhere near me, that is — when I know it should be you. It would be even harder for me to pretend I want to be his friend. I'm not a phony."

Ben said, "I know that."

"I should be catching passes from you," he said. "Then the season would be as fun as it's supposed to be."

Ben kept trying to find fun ways for football to be more fun to Shawn, but to also get him throwing better under pressure. On Friday, Ben's dad hung a tire from the maple tree at McBain. When Shawn got there after school, Ben rushed him like a crazy man, and told Shawn they were staying out there until he could either put the ball through the tire, or at least hit it.

"You're sure this is fun?" Shawn said.

Ben said, "Hey, you think it's fun for me being a defensive tackle?"

Lily showed up on Friday just as Shawn was leaving. They knew each other a little from school. But just a little.

"Can I ask you one serious question?" Lily said, before she started going out for passes.

"Like I could stop you even if I wanted."

Lily said, "Does it bother you that you're trying to help Shawn get better at something you're already better at than *him*?"

Ben grinned. "It did at first, no lie. But I just keep telling myself that if it helps the team, it's worth it."

"All about the team with you," she said, "isn't it?"

"Well, *yeah*," he said.

"Boy, there's something about this guy Sam and Coop really don't like," she said.

"You're *kidding*," Ben said, "I hadn't picked up on that."

Even though Shawn always seemed to throw pretty well at

practice, Ben thought he could see improvement out of him as the week went along. And Thursday's scrimmage ended with him pulling the ball down on a busted pass play, running to his right, avoiding a linebacker, hitting Kevin Nolti with a strike in the middle of the field. Doing what Ben wanted him to do in games, reacting instead of thinking too much.

Ben and Coop and Sam walked off the field together.

"You gotta admit, he's looking better," Ben said. "You gotta give me that."

"In practice," Coop said.

"What about the thing that coaches are always telling us, that you practice like you play?" Ben said.

"Shawn doesn't," Sam said.

"Even if he is your new best friend," Coop said.

"You know that's not right," Ben said.

"I'm right about Shawn until he proves me wrong," Sam Brown said.

Ben wanted Shawn to prove Sam wrong. And Coop. But for now, Ben knew Sam *was* right. Even though they'd only been playing town football since the Bantam Division, they all knew something by now: There *were* guys who could practice like total champions, just never bring that with them to Saturday, when you started keeping score.

Coop's mom was driving them all home tonight. On their way to the parking lot a few minutes later, Coach O'Brien and Shawn were up ahead of them, Coach with his arm around Shawn's shoulders, talking away, Shawn nodding his head up and down, as if to keep up with whatever he was being told.

His dad coaching all the way to the car.

12

Hewitt was a small town, even smaller than Rockwell, about twenty minutes away, never known for its football teams, from Pop Warner through high school. Last season, in fact, the Hewitt Giants had been everybody's *favorite* opponent in the Bantam Division, not winning a single game.

The Rams had played them in their second-to-last game, Ben running for three touchdowns and Sam going fifty yards for another score on an end-around. The final was 26–0 and could have been worse — *would* have been worse — if Coach Bucci didn't order them to basically eat the ball the whole fourth quarter.

During warm-ups, Coop said to Ben, "I still think they should do the right thing and change their name."

"To what?"

"Well, anything but Giants," he said. "Because, dude, they're, like, the opposite of giants. What did they call the little people in that Jack Black movie we thought was so terrible?"

Ben laughed. Sometimes he couldn't help himself with Coop.

"What's so funny?" Coop said.

"You," Ben said. "And you're talking about *Gulliver's Travels*, right?"

"Yeah," Coop said. "And that's supposed to be funny?"

"It's not always *what* you say, it's the way you say it," Ben said. "You do know that was a pretty famous book, right?"

"Whatever," Coop said. "And so I can't remember what the little people were called, big deal."

"Lilliputians," Ben said.

"So that's what these guys should be called, then," Coop said. "The Hewitt Lilliputians."

"Coming from a mental giant like yourself, that would probably hurt their feelings."

"Is that a shot at me?" Coop said.

"No *way*," Ben said. "But hey? Just because they stunk last year doesn't mean they will this year. And it's not like we ripped it up last week."

Coop looked down the field to where the Hewitt players were doing their own stretching.

"Same old, same old," he said. "They still look like little Giants to me."

Only the Giants came out playing big, taking the opening kickoff and marching all the way down the field, the quarterback being a lot better than Ben remembered, the team making one first down after another. They finally ended up with a first and goal from the two and the quarterback walked in from there, then threw for a two-point conversion. Just like that it was 8–0, Rockwell not even having run a play yet.

"Okay, so maybe they don't stink," Coop said.

"Man," Sam said, "you don't miss *any*thing."

Ben said, "Let's do to them what they just did to us."

But the Rams could only make one first down on their first series, having to punt after Shawn held the ball too long on third down and got sacked. Got up talking to himself.

The Bad Shawn.

Coming off the field Shawn came over to Ben and in a low voice said, "I froze."

One bad play and it was as if all the good work they'd done during the week was out the window.

"No," Ben said, "you didn't freeze. You just got sacked. There's a difference."

He wanted to add, *Suck it up.* But didn't.

Even now it was like there was a Good Shawn and a Bad Shawn. The good one showed up on their next series, like he'd shown up late for the game, completing five passes in a row, mostly short ones.

But then held on to the ball a little too long again on third down, tried to scramble, got brought down short of the first-down marker.

The Giants started driving the ball again near the end of the half, looking as if they might go up two touchdowns. That was before their quarterback was the one rushing a throw under a pretty heavy blitz, trying to force the ball to his tight end, getting hardly anything on the throw. Sam Brown, who played safety when Coach would put him in on defense, stepped in front of the kid on the left sideline, picked the ball off, and then ran away as if a mean dog was chasing him.

Shawn pitched it to Ben for the conversion, Ben got to the outside before anybody could touch him, and even though the Rams had done hardly anything on offense so far, the game was 8–8, which is the way it stayed until halftime.

When Coach O'Brien gathered the team around him, he acted as if they had the Hewitt Giants right where they wanted them. It was one of those times when Ben couldn't really understand why Shawn felt so much pressure from his dad, because Coach O'Brien didn't just want Shawn to do well, he wanted them all to do well. Believed they *would* do well. And no matter what the situation, did his own best to convince them they were *going* to do well.

He was like that now behind their bench at Hewitt, kneeling in the grass, like he was more excited than any of his players to get to the second half.

"We're fine," he said. "More than fine, actually. You can see the kids on the other side of the field are playing their best game. But that's gonna be a problem for them the rest of the way, because we haven't nearly played our best yet. Sam just picked us up with a big play to get us going and I'm telling you, we are ready to roll."

Then he told them that they were going to come out throwing in the second half, for the simple reason that he didn't think Hewitt would be expecting it. And also, he said, because he was sure the passing game was ready to click.

"I know something the other guys don't know," Coach said. "My quarterback can *really* throw, and I've got a bunch of different guys who can catch."

He reached over, tapped the top of Shawn's head lightly, like he was knocking on a door. "You good with that?" he said to his son.

Ben heard Shawn say in a loud voice, "*So* good."

Ben thought: *He sounds like he's trying to convince himself.*

"All I needed to hear from my boy," he said. "We'll throw and that will set up our running game later when it's time to put this baby to bed. That's the way my friend Peyton Manning has always done it."

Ben thought: *Now we'll see if Shawn can do it here the way he's been doing it all week with me at McBain Field.*

"This should be interesting, airing it out," Sam said before Ben jogged back to receive the kickoff.

"Shawn's going to surprise us," Ben said. "Just watch."

Sam grinned. "You really need to work on that bad attitude of yours."

Ben shot straight up the middle, returned the kick to the Rams' forty-five-yard line. Shawn went to work from there.

The passing game started clicking again, just the way Coach said it would. The line, starting with Coop at center, was giving Shawn all day to throw now. So he did. Short to Ben on the right sideline. To Sam over the middle. Then Sam again on a slant. No pressure now, at least from the Hewitt defense. For the first time, in the second game of the season, Shawn looked like the quarterback his dad said he was, had told Ben he was.

The Good Shawn. Playing like the quarterback his dad wanted him to be.

He completed four more passes in a row. On first and goal from the Giants' nine-yard line, Sam drew a lot of attention in the defensive backfield going over the middle, Ben curled in behind him, wide open. Shawn almost underthrew him, maybe because Ben was so open. But Ben scooped the ball up before it hit the ground, turned, and ran untouched into the end zone.

Shawn *did* underthrow Darrelle for the conversion, giving Hewitt's middle linebacker time to knock the ball down. But the Rams had the lead now, 14–8. As they all ran off the field Ben got alongside Shawn and said, "I *told* you that you could do it."

"Long way to go," Shawn said.

"So what?" Ben said. "When you're playing well, you want to play all day."

Ben was hoping they could shut Hewitt down, get the offense the ball right back, make this a game when Shawn wouldn't be required to make plays at the end.

It didn't work out that way.

The Giants were the ones who came right back, another long drive, mixing passes and runs, always seeming to have the Rams off balance. Ben was in at cornerback now, and briefly saved a touchdown by tipping a ball away from one of the Giants' wide receivers at the last second. But then the Giants' quarterback ran it in from the ten on a quarterback draw, and then their fullback ran straight up the middle for the conversion.

It was 16–14.

Them.

Nobody did much on offense after that. Shawn missed some open receivers, but so did the Hewitt quarterback. So the game stayed 16–14 into the fourth quarter. With about six minutes left, the Rams began a long drive that started deep in their own territory. But on third down from Hewitt's thirty, Shawn led Sam too much down the sideline. Sam got a hand on the ball, tried to tip it to himself. But when it looked as if he might do that, he got hit from the side, the ball popping straight up in the air.

When it came down, it came down into the hands of their safety.

Hewitt ball, two minutes left.

And maybe game over.

Ben ran straight for Shawn and said, "Not your fault."

"Did somebody else throw that ball?" he said.

"You were just unlucky," Ben said. "*We* were unlucky."

"My dad always tells me you make your own luck in sports," Shawn said.

He ran off the field, ran straight to his favorite spot at the end of the bench, like he was trying to crawl into a hole. Ben stayed on the field, Coach O'Brien having moved him to safety, Ben back there with Sam. It was where Ben liked it best on defense, he and Sam were a great team at the back of the defense, each one knowing where the other was going to be without having to talk about it.

Sam said, "We can't let them run out the clock."

"No," Ben said. "Because we are *not* going to 0–2."

"You want to make a play, or should I?" Sam said.

As it turned out, they both did.

On third down, the Hewitt halfback broke into the clear, running free into the Rams' defensive backfield. But Sam closed in on him from one side, Ben from the other. Then Sam went in low on the kid, and as he did, Ben went in high, swinging his right hand at the ball the way Coach O'Brien had taught them.

Knocking it loose.

A lot of players seemed to show up at the party then, fighting for the ball. Too late. Sam Brown had it and nobody was getting it away from him. Rams' ball on the Hewitt twenty-nine-yard line. A minute and eight seconds showing on the clock.

Darrelle brought the first down play in from the bench. A simple post pattern to Sam. Go down about ten yards, cut hard to the middle of the field, find some open space.

Sam did, two steps ahead of the cornerback covering him, the safety just standing there as Sam put on a burst, like he could, and ran right past him.

Shawn threw the ball so far behind him it hit the Hewitt safety who'd made the interception on Sam a few minutes earlier right between the numbers.

Only the kid was so startled he dropped it, going to his knees afterward and giving the ground a good pounding, as if he knew he might have just fumbled away his team's chance to beat Rockwell.

Second and ten.

Ben figured it was okay to exhale now.

Kevin Nolti brought in the next play, "Swing 22," Ben's number, a quick pass to him coming out of the backfield, Brian McAuley blocking ahead of him, trying to get Ben to the outside. As they broke the huddle Ben said to Shawn, "Just throw me the ball, I'll do the rest."

"If I can," Shawn said.

He was so tight it was like he could barely open his mouth to get the words out.

Shawn only had to throw the ball about five yards. Still he almost missed Ben, Shawn not throwing the ball so much as trying to push it through the air. It was more a little pop-up than a pass, Ben worried that the ball was hanging up in the air so long somebody might blast in to pick it off the way the Midvale guy had the week before.

No one did. Ben finally wrapped his arms around the ball, saw Brian block Hewitt's outside linebacker to the inside, broke to the outside himself, didn't get knocked out of bounds until he'd made it all the way to their six-yard line.

First and goal.

Still plenty of time.

Then Ben got stopped for no gain on first down. Same with Darrelle on second. Coach O'Brien called time-out. Thirty-one seconds on the clock, Ben thinking: We waited all week and we're pretty much right back where we were at the end of the Midvale game.

Just down two this time.

Coach sent in a pass, to Sam, a little fade route where Sam gave a quick head fake to the cornerback covering him, then cut behind him to the right corner of the end zone.

Shawn gave everybody the play, the snap count, clapped his hands. But before he got down behind Coop, he turned to Ben, as if wanting to tell him one last thing before the ball was snapped.

Just not anything Ben wanted to hear in that moment.

"I'm choking my brains out," the Bad Shawn said.

Sam would joke that way sometimes in a game, never meaning it.

Shawn did.

"Don't," Ben said. "Sam is so good it's, like, ridiculous. You get it anywhere near him, trust me, he *will* go up and get it."

But the Hewitt coach crossed them up and called for an all-out blitz, sending in one of his safeties and all three of his linebackers. Total fire drill. Like the whole Hewitt defense was trying to throw the kind of scare into Shawn that Ben's dad had when he'd been the designated pass rusher at McBain Field, trying to get Shawn ready for a moment in the game like this.

Only he wasn't ready.

When he saw Hewitt uniforms coming at him from all directions, he didn't even try to run. He just panicked, didn't give Sam enough time to make his cut, threw the ball high and wild and out of the end zone.

Fourth down.

Like they were down to their last out in baseball.

Coach O'Brien was smiling on the sideline as he sent in the play with Kevin Nolti, pumping his fist at the Rams. "Let's do this!" he yelled.

This play was called "Sneak 22." Ben again. He was supposed to stay home and block while Shawn rolled to his left, the side of the field where Sam had lined up. But as soon as Ben threw his block, he was supposed to jog to his right, almost as if he wasn't even in the play.

Then Shawn was supposed to turn and throw him the ball and — if the play worked the way Coach O'Brien thought it would — Ben would run from there into the end zone.

Easy throw for Shawn to make, tough play for the defense to read. Ben thought: *It shouldn't have come down to one play. But if it had to, I'm glad the play is to me.*

Shawn dropped back. Hewitt blitzed again. Coop leveled one of their tackles, Ben put a good low block on a linebacker. Then he was out in the right flat. All alone.

Now.

One of the Hewitt corners, the one covering Brian underneath the goalposts, had spotted him. But he was hanging back with Brian for now, not wanting to leave *him* wide open in the back of the end zone.

Shawn waited the way he'd been told to on this play, then suddenly turned toward Ben, brought his arm forward, Ben seeing the tight spiral come out of his hand.

Ben decided to give one quick look up the field and when he did he saw the cornerback on Brian starting to run toward him.

All it took. When he turned back for the ball it was already on him, and he wasn't ready for it. At the worst possible moment, Ben was the one who turned out to be too anxious, wanting to start running before he had the ball, wanting to get to the end zone, wanting to win the game for his team.

Wanting way too much for this quarterback to throw the winning pass.

The ball went through Ben's hands, fell to the ground incomplete as the Rams fell to 0–2.

Ben didn't even remember dropping to his knees.

But there he was in the grass now, the ball in front of him, still not believing what had just happened, not believing the game had ended the way it had, that he'd lost it all by himself.

He always wanted the ball in his hands at the end of a close game, in any sport.

It just wasn't supposed to go *through* his hands.

Not like this, not now.

He was aware of a lot of yelling from behind him, knowing it was from the Hewitt Giants, who weren't the worst team in the league anymore.

Because we are, Ben thought.

He stayed where he was, his knees on the five-yard line, hands on his thigh pads, still staring at the ball on the field in front of him.

"Hey."

Ben looked up and saw Sam Brown. Next to Sam was Coop. His wingmen. That's what Coop said they were, even before they started calling themselves the Core Four.

Sam put out his hand. Ben reached for it. Sam pulled him to his feet, saying, "Come on, we're pretty much done here."

Sam was grinning at him, helmet already off, holding it in his left hand.

"I can't believe I dropped it," Ben said.

"It happens," Coop said, "even to you, a guy who's a total dog most of the time."

"Dog" to Coop was high praise. You just had to know that his vocabulary was sometimes upside down from everybody else's. "Stupid" was good, too.

"Today I was a mutt," Ben said.

"Coop's right," Sam said, "even though I don't believe I just said that. Happens to everybody and now it happened to you. What about the time your guy, Aaron Rodgers, coughed it up in overtime in the playoffs? The guy from the Cardinals ran it in and the Pack's season was over."

"Rodgers got hit," Ben said.

"His season was still over," Sam said. "Ours isn't."

"You sure?" Ben said.

"Who's the guy always saying we win as a team and lose as a team?" Coop said. "Wait, I know. It's *you*."

"Not today," Ben said. "Today it was all me."

"Right, you're the worst player ever," Sam said. "Now let's go shake hands and see how fast we can get out of Hewitt."

Ben looked around for Shawn, wanting to apologize for dropping a sure game-winner. In a big spot, Shawn had stepped up and made the play. Been the player he wanted to be.

Ben wanted to make sure he knew it wasn't his fault that the Rams had lost.

Everybody else was already in the line. That included Shawn this time, up at the front, right ahead of his dad. Ben and Sam and Coop fell in, went through the motions even though they didn't feel like it, kept mumbling "Great game" and "Way to go" to the Hewitt guys, just wanting this part of the day to be over the way the game was.

Then go listen to Coach try to put a smiley face on this week's killer loss.

Shawn was about halfway to their bench when Ben caught up with him. "Dude," he said. "I am *so* stinking sorry."

Shawn stopped, took off his helmet now, staring at Ben at first as if he was just some random guy from the other team.

"Thanks," he said.

"*Thanks?*"

"Yeah," Shawn said. "You promised to be my friend, and just now you were."

Ben said, "I don't get it."

"No, I feel a lot better now," Shawn said.

Ben starting to hear the sarcasm in his voice.

"Yeah," Shawn O'Brien said, "I feel a *whole* lot better today knowing I'm not the biggest choker on the team."

Ben opened his mouth, closed it, not sure what to say to that. Now the Bad Shawn wasn't just in at quarterback, talking to himself after a bad play, he was standing right in front of Ben.

Ben didn't know Sam and Coop were still with him, but heard Sam's voice now.

"Shut up," he said.

Ben said to Sam, "Let it go."

"No," Sam said.

He stepped up so that he was on Ben's right shoulder. Coop was on the other side.

Sam said to Shawn, "You must be joking, calling somebody else a choker."

"What, he didn't choke?" Shawn said. "What game were you watching? A five-year-old could have caught that ball."

"I'm starting to think maybe a five-year-old threw it," Coop said.

"You're a real team guy, O'Brien, you know that?" Sam said.

Shawn looked at all of them.

"Yeah," Shawn said. "You should probably talk to the coach and get him to throw me off it."

Then he turned and walked away. Sam started to go after him, Ben put a hand on his arm and stopped him, not wanting this to be any worse than it already was.

If that was possible.

"Let him go," Ben said.

"I told you he was a jerk," Coop said.

Ben wasn't sure what Shawn was right now. Or who he was. Or why the guy he'd been working out with all week had said what he said, acted the way he had. All Ben knew was that he'd come into the season wanting to get to know Shawn better and unfortunately, now he did.

It was only four o'clock when the bus Coach O'Brien had rented for the team out of his own pocket turned into the parking lot at Rockwell Middle School. Even though most of the parents had traveled to Hewitt to watch the game, Coach still wanted the players to return home from road trips — even short ones — together.

"There are all kinds of ways to learn how to be a real team," he said, "and one of them is on the ride home. Win or lose."

Shawn sat with his dad in the first seat behind the driver. Ben and Sam and Coop were all the way in back.

Sam hardly ever lost his temper, it was why Ben was surprised to see him come at Shawn the way he did after the game. Usually it was Coop who acted like a hothead, and that was the Coop they had gotten for the whole ride back, Coop keeping his voice low, but still going on and on about Shawn, and finding different ways to call him a scrub.

If "dog" was the biggest compliment you could get out of Coop, "scrub" was the biggest insult. He was still at it even as the bus pulled to a stop.

"Total scrub," Coop said as the guys started to file off the bus, "from the scrub Hall of Fame. If you want to grow up to be a scrub someday, you put his picture up on your wall."

Ben said, "I think he just needed somebody to be mad at."

Now Sam got hot all over again.

"For the last time," Sam said, "stop defending this guy. He sold you out for one dropped ball."

Ben could see how steamed he still was, so he let it go, but not before Sam said, "You know how Coach says you gotta learn to lose before you learn to win sometimes? It's gonna be no problem for his son. Because he's a complete loser already."

Before they got into their parents' cars, Sam and Coop asked Ben if he wanted them to come over once they got out of their gear. Ben said he'd give them a shout-out before dinner, or maybe right after, but right now he wanted to go chill by himself.

Not an option, as it turned out.

When he got home, there was Lily sitting on his front porch waiting for him.

From the backseat Ben said to his parents, "Okay, which one of you called her and told her how the game ended?"

Both his mom and dad swore they didn't.

"Then she definitely does have a sixth sense," Ben said. "Or a *sick* sense. Girl's a freak."

"Just speaking from the female perspective," Beth McBain said, "I'm hoping you can find a better way to describe Lily's psychic powers if you mention them to her."

Ben had taken off his shoulder pads and jersey and cleats in the car, was just wearing a T-shirt now, along with his football pants and socks. Lily was in sneakers and so when she came down the steps to greet him, she seemed even taller compared to Ben than she usually was.

Figures, he thought.

In the biggest moment of the season so far, he had come up small. *So* small.

"Okay," Ben said, "who ratted me out?"

Lily smiled, making him feel better right away even though he didn't want to, he wanted to stay bummed.

"Ratted you out on what?"

"That I blew the game for us."

"Oh," Lily said, "*that*."

"Yeah. That."

Lily said, "I thought you meant somebody had told me something *major*, not the ending to some silly old football game."

"Not silly to me."

"Yeah," Lily said, "it's a shame that your season had to end that way." Still smiling. "Oh, wait," she said, slapping her forehead now, "the season *didn't* come to an end. Or the world!"

"You didn't tell me who told you."

"Well, if you *must* know, Justin's parents couldn't go to the game, but he needed to tell them when pickup was. So he borrowed a phone and called home and Ella" — Justin's sister — "answered. And Justin told her and she called and told me and here I am."

"Here you are," Ben said. "But I don't want to talk about the game."

"Me *neither*!"

Ben couldn't help himself. She sounded so relieved it made him laugh.

"C'mon," Lily said, pulling him by the arm, "let's go sit on the swings. I know that always makes me feel better about everything."

"Just let me get out of these stupid football clothes," he said. "Take me one minute."

"Stupid clothes for a stupid game, if you ask me."

Ben managed a smile now. "Just keep talking, Lils, you won't even notice I'm gone."

He ran up to his bedroom, put on his favorite Packers Super Bowl T-shirt, shorts, sneakers, thinking to himself:

Maybe I didn't want to be alone nearly as much as I thought I did.

Or maybe he just wanted to be alone except for Lily.

They walked to the far end of McBain Field, stopped before they got to the basketball court, each of them taking a swing. Their moms had pushed them in these swings when they were little.

They each gave themselves a push with their legs, quietly rocked back and forth in the air.

When they took a break Lily said, "What?"

"I didn't say anything."

"Didn't have to. *Never* have to. So go ahead and talk about whatever it is you're not talking about, even if it is the silly game you said you *weren't* going to talk about."

He took a deep breath, let it out.

"Okay," Ben said. "If we had won today, we'd have one win and one loss, and we'd be fine. But now we're not fine because we're 0–2 and might have no chance of playing in the championship game."

"And it's all your fault."

"Well, *yeah*, now that you mention it."

"You really are such an idiot sometimes."

"No argument. Clumsy one, too."

105

"I don't know anything about your idiotic game and I know

that your team probably wouldn't have had any chance to win without you."

"Doesn't matter why you lost. Just that you lost. A famous coach said that one time."

"Blah blah blah," Lily said with a wave of her hand. "Now what else aren't you telling me?"

Why fight it? Girl was a total mind-reading freak.

At least with me she is, Ben thought.

"Actually, there is one other thing," he said, and told her what Shawn said to him when the game was over.

"He really said that?" she said. "To *you*?"

Ben nodded.

"The guy you tried to help not be so much of a choker himself?"

"Sam and Coop didn't want to hear it, but I said he just needed to be hacked off at somebody and picked me. Guys do that sometimes."

"You don't."

"Sure I do," Ben said, grinning at her. "I just don't try it in front of you."

"No, McBain," she said. "You don't. You're a boy, everybody knows boys are a little slow sometimes. But you're not mean. You're *never* mean. And what he said to you was plain old mean."

Then Lily Wyatt said, "Something I am going to point out to *that* boy on Monday."

"No," Ben said. "Sam and Shawn nearly went at it after the game. But this is between him and me."

"Why *were* you so nice to him in the first place?" she said, cocking that eyebrow like she could.

"I already told you."

"Right. I know what you *told* me."

"I was just trying to help a guy out, help him get better."

"How's that workin' out for you so far?"

"Hey," Ben said, "nobody wants to get called a gagger. But it's not like he was lying, at least today. You can see he's all worried about letting his dad down and today he snapped after I let him down."

"You just dropped a ball," Lily said.

"Can *we* drop *this*?" Ben said.

"Done," she said.

Then she gave him her best smile so far and said, "See how easy it is to drop stuff?"

Ben still thought Shawn might try to call and apologize on Sunday for what he said. But he didn't. Didn't apologize at school on Monday.

So just like that, things had changed between them.

Because of one dropped pass.

They didn't talk about it on the phone, didn't talk about it at school, didn't talk about it at practice. It wasn't as if they were *not* talking. They didn't ignore each other in the hall or on the field. But now it was as if the good stuff that started to happen between them — that day over pizza, then at Shawn's field when he shared his secret about not wanting to be a quarterback, at McBain Field — had never happened.

Like they'd de-friended each other.

Anybody watching them at practice before their next game, against Parkerville, wouldn't have thought anything had changed between them. Ben knew better. So did Sam and Coop. And Lily, because Ben would tell her all about it when he got home.

"You gotta stop worrying about this guy," Sam said to Ben at The Rock on Saturday morning, the two of them first to show up for the Parkerville game. "You keep making excuses for him, but I keep telling *you*: If he could chump on you like that, he was never going to be your friend."

"Maybe he doesn't know how to be a friend any more than he knows how to be a quarterback," Ben said. "Maybe he just has to learn how."

Sam said, "Give it up." Held up a hand and said, "I know, I know, he's our teammate."

"He is."

"And he had a chance to act like one, and didn't," Sam said. "Maybe that was the real choke job last Saturday, a bigger one, because being a friend is more important than winning a game."

Ben said, "How about we just talk about the game we're going to play and not the one we played last week."

"Now you're making sense," Sam said. "I am *so* down with that."

Ben knew something: Once Sam dug in, try moving him. Especially when he thought someone had been disloyal. Sam cared a lot about sports, as much as Ben did. But he didn't say things just to sound good. He really did care about friendship and loyalty more.

That was his real Bro Code, even if he didn't talk about his as much as Coop did.

Ben did bring it all back to football now, and not just because he wanted to change the subject from Shawn O'Brien.

He said, "My dad says you're never as bad as you look when you're losing and never as good as you look when you're winning. So how about we find out today if that's true about the winning part?"

Sam reached out and tapped him some fist, and then ran down the field and Ben threw him the ball he'd been holding in his right hand. And just like that, it wasn't last Saturday anymore. It was this Saturday. This game against Parkerville. The only one that mattered.

But he knew that the Rams getting their first win of the season wasn't going to be easy. The Parkerville Patriots would probably have won the Bantam championship the year before if their quarterback, Robbie Burnett, hadn't broken his wrist with three games to go. Robbie had been the best quarterback in the league last season, as big as Shawn, with an even better arm. And Robbie was much better running the ball. The whole package. He really was a born quarterback. Last year's Patriots had only lost once before Robbie got hurt, then never won another game after he did.

He was back now, though. According to Coop, who had a cousin on the Parkerville team, Robbie was throwing and running better than ever and the Patriots had started their season with two straight wins.

"You can even tell how good he is watching him warm up," Coop said.

"We're still winning today," Ben said.

"Yeah," Coop said, "if *our* quarterback shows up."

"Maybe today's the day Shawn surprises us," Ben said.

"You mean he's going to be a good player *and* a good guy?" Coop said.

"Football's not a game of one-on-one," Ben said, "our quarterback against theirs."

Coop walked away, saying, "Good thing."

When Coach O'Brien spoke to them behind the bench right before the game, he kept things brief. And got Ben to thinking all over again about how even as he liked Shawn less and less, he liked his dad more and more.

"We're getting better," Coach said. "I know you still can't see that in that left-hand column where the wins go. But I can see it. I see it in the way you guys fight, how hard you work at practice. And I can see the thing coaches always look for when a team is scuffling: I see the way you're hanging together."

Coop and Ben were in the back of the circle and now Coop whispered, "Well, some of us are."

Ben put an elbow into his ribs to shut him up.

Coach said, "So we start our season all over again today. Everybody on this team just try to win a battle on each play with somebody on the other side of the line of scrimmage. Do that the whole game and no way those guys beat us."

He waved as a way of bringing them in closer.

"Listen, I don't like to make guarantees," he said. "I'm not Rex Ryan of the Jets. But there *is* a method to what seems like Coach Ryan's madness. He makes his guarantees to let his players know he believes in them. I believe in you. We're winning today. Like I hear you guys say to each other all the time: Hundred percent."

Then it was 20–0 at the half.

For Parkerville.

•   •   •

When they were coming off the field, everybody acting as if the game was already over, feeling as if they were behind more than they actually were the way Robbie Burnett was torching them, Coop said, "Hey, I've got a guarantee."

Sam said, "Do me a favor: Don't be funny right now. Which for you really isn't a challenge, now that I think about it."

"Wasn't gonna be funny," Coop said.

Ben said, "So, what's your guarantee?"

"That the only way we come back on these guys is if their quarterback comes and plays for us the second half and ours goes over and plays for them."

Ben had been right about one thing with Shawn: He *had* surprised them. By playing even worse, after a decent start, than he had over the first two games.

He did make some solid throws early, to Sam, to Darrelle, to Justin, and the Rams were driving on their first possession of the game. But then on a first down from the Patriots' nineteen-yard line, he floated one to Sam on the sideline that hung in the air like a kite, the Patriots' outside linebacker stepped in and returned it all the way down the sideline for a touchdown.

It was mostly Robbie after that, running and passing, making their defense look bad, like he'd moved up to a new league this year but the guys trying to stop him should still be in Bantam. He led his team on two long touchdown drives and would have had one more if his fullback hadn't fumbled on a first-and-goal play from the three-yard line.

The Rams had one last chance to get on the board right before halftime, Ben wide open in the end zone after they'd pretty much used running plays to move down the field. But Shawn — who hadn't completed a single pass the whole second quarter — missed him by a good five yards, the ball ending up in the hands of the Patriots' free safety instead.

When they got to the sideline, Shawn came over to Ben and said, "Try running the right route next time."

Loud enough for everybody on the team to hear. Probably loud enough for *both* teams to hear.

In a quieter voice Ben said, "What?"

"You heard me."

"Actually, I think my mom and dad heard you," Ben said, not able to stop himself from at least saying that.

"I was expecting you to cut to the corner," Shawn said.

Ben didn't want to get into this with him, not now, not down three touchdowns, not in front of the whole team. Knowing at the same time he'd never call a teammate out like this.

All he said was, "The play was for me to run to an open spot."

"Next time try to fake out the defense, not me," Shawn said, and walked away from him to go get a drink of Gatorade.

Ben wondered what Coach would have done if he'd heard what Shawn said, but he hadn't, he was down talking to the refs, there had been some problem with the clock right at the end of the half.

When Coach jogged back over and got with the Rams, he didn't talk about the way his own quarterback had played, just focused on Robbie Burnett, who'd thrown for one touchdown and run for another, explained what they needed to do to stop him in the second half if they were going to get back in the game.

"We're gonna start blitzing him every chance we get," Coach O'Brien said, "see if we can get him out of his comfort zone that way. It's a risky way to play, especially against a kid that good, and one who can run around the way he can. But we gotta try something."

On offense, he said, they were going to come out throwing, Coach acting in that moment as if the incompletions they'd all seen, the two interceptions Shawn had thrown, hadn't happened.

Coop whispered, "Is there some other game he's been watching?"

Ben elbowed him again, even though he knew Cooper Manley was just saying out loud what everybody else on the team had to be thinking.

Why keep throwing when your quarterback couldn't today?

Coach O'Brien wrapped up his talk this way: "They scored 20? We just gotta find a way to hold them there and score 21 ourselves."

As they came out of the circle and took the field, Coop said, "Does he think the other team is going home?"

"If you give up on me, or even *act* like you're giving up," Ben said, "I will give you a beatdown."

It got a grin out of Coop. "Worse than the one Robbie Burnett is giving us?"

114

But they still couldn't make a dent on Parkerville in the third quarter. Once the Rams started blitzing, at least making Robbie start to miss a little, their coach seemed content to have them just keep running the ball, obviously thinking that the way the Rams had looked on offense, twenty points was more than enough to win.

Maybe thinking three points was enough to win.

Shawn did manage to complete a couple of short passes. But when the Rams started to get a good drive going, he threw another interception, missing Justin badly.

Finally on the last play of the quarter, the Rams caught what felt like their first break of the day. Robbie dropped back to throw, looking like he wanted to cross them up, throw long, close out the Rams once and for all. But he never saw Sam Brown coming all the way from safety, flying in from his blind side, knocking the ball out of Robbie's hand, recovering it himself at the Rams' thirty-five-yard line.

Quarter over.

Even though Sam's play might have kept them in the game, Ben looked around and saw the Rams hanging their heads more now than they had at the half, as if Sam's play hadn't kept them in anything, as if the game really were over, whether they had the ball back or not.

Ben went and got himself a quick drink of water, was standing with his back to the field when he felt the tap on his shoulder.

Coach.

"Listen, I know it's a lousy spot. But I'm gonna give you some snaps. I just told Shawn."

At first Ben wasn't sure he'd heard him right. Looked down the bench and saw Shawn at the other end of it, hands on hips, glaring at his dad. Or Ben. Or both of them.

Ben said, "You're putting me in . . . at quarterback?"

"I am. Shake things up a little."

Sam Brown was behind Coach, hearing what Ben was hearing. Throwing a fist in the air. Not caring if the rest of the team saw.

Ben could feel his heart pounding. Wanted to throw a fist himself and yell, *Yes*. But he just kept nodding his head, taking in everything Coach was saying to him about playing as if the game were 0–0, somehow convincing his teammates that they still had a chance.

When Coach walked away, Sam and Coop were there, both giving Ben quick low fives.

It was Coop who said, "Welcome to McBain Field."

"At last," Sam said.

Coach O'Brien sent Ben in with the first three plays, all passes, the first to Sam.

Perfect.

Ben wasn't looking to deliver any pep talks in the huddle like the one Coach had just given him. Just looking to deliver good passes. So he knelt down, looked up at his teammates, gave them the play and the snap count, then just added one thing:

"Let's play like we're in the street, and we're not ready to go home yet." They couldn't see him through his face mask, grinning at them as he said, "Even though it *is* getting pretty late."

The first throw was supposed to be a simple one, Ben rolling to his right as if he were going to run the ball, then pulling up and throwing to Sam in the right flat. But he nearly blew it over Sam's head, too geeked up to make the first throw perfect.

Only his buddy Sam Brown wasn't going to let him start with an incompletion. Sam went up as high as he could, brought the ball down with his big hands, broke a tackle as he turned upfield, ran all the way to midfield.

First down.

"Thank you," Ben said when Sam got back to the huddle.

"We're a team," Sam said. "Remember?"

The second play was supposed to be a screen to Darrelle on the left, but the Patriots' middle linebacker saw it coming, breaking through the blocking in front of Darrelle as if it wasn't there. Ben was barely able to pull the ball down in time, sprint to his right. As he did, he saw Sam coming from all the way across the field, running to an open spot near the sideline. This time Ben's throw, on the run, wasn't high. Just money. Sam kept both feet inbounds like a pro. Twelve yards on the play. Another first down, at the Parkerville thirty-eight-yard line.

Like that, they were moving.

The third pass was supposed to be another short pass to Darrelle. He was supposed to run to his right like he was blocking for Ben, then just slip into the defensive backfield for a little five-yard throw, see if he could make something out of it from there.

But before Ben brought his arm up to throw, he saw the linebacker coming up to cover Darrelle slip and fall. When Darrelle turned for the ball, Ben just used his left arm to wave him deep. Like this really was street ball now, and they were both making the play up as they went along.

The kind of play where Ben had always been at his best.

Darrelle took off. Ben could see the rush coming at him from the side, had to turn the ball loose before he was ready, and before Darrelle was ready. So he put some extra air under the ball, hoping Darrelle would run under it. Hoping he hadn't led him by too much.

The Parkerville safety, a fast guy, tried to recover, catch up with Darrelle before it was too late. But it already was. Ben hadn't led him too much. Darrelle ran under the ball at about the Parkerville fifteen, bobbling it slightly as it came down into his hands, looking as if he were about to drop it. Ben's heart dropped at the same time. But he kept watching as Darrelle pressed the ball to his chest with both hands, ran the rest of the way to the end zone without anybody putting a hand on him.

They were on the board.

Ben wasn't sure what his best time might be in a forty-yard dash. But by the time Darrelle turned around, Ben was on him better than the Parkerville safety had been, halfway into a full, flying chest bump.

"What's good?" Darrelle said.

"Us," Ben said.

"You're right," Darrelle said. "I'm *not* ready to go home yet."

The conversion happened to be a play Ben and Sam loved to mess around with at McBain, even though there was no way Coach O'Brien could have known that. Ben just took a one-step drop, lobbed the ball over the defensive linemen and over everybody, like he was Dwayne Wade firing up a lob for LeBron to dunk.

The Parkerville cornerback on Sam could jump. Just not like Sam Brown could jump. When he came down with the ball in the corner of the end zone, he had both feet inbounds, by a lot, and now the score was Parkerville 20, Rockwell 8.

Still ten minutes left at The Rock.

Coop came over to Ben and said he had a thought he wanted to share.

"Thoughts are good," Ben said, "especially for you."

"So you want to hear it?"

"Absolutely!"

Coop said, "Let's play like total dogs the rest of the way."

"Woof, woof," Ben said.

Sam said he was pretty much all in with that, too. And so was Coach O'Brien, as it turned out, telling them on the sideline that he wanted Sam to try an onside kick.

Coach told them fast, told them without even looking at Sam, wanting everything to look normal, not wanting it to look as if he was giving them special instructions and tip off the Patriots coach on what was coming next.

"Just bounce that sucker up the field like you do in practice," Coach said.

"Got it," Sam said, starting back out on the field.

"Whichever side is easier for you," Coach said, tossing Sam his kicking tee, then saying to Ben, "You go with him," even though Ben wasn't usually on the kickoff team.

When Sam took the ball from the ref he said to Ben, "Going to you."

"Thought you might."

"Right or left?"

"Right."

"Do me a favor?" Sam said quietly, setting the ball on the tee. "Stay onside. *Very* key for an onside kick. We're only gonna get one shot at this."

The Parkerville coach either sensed something was coming, or was just playing it safe, putting a lot of receivers and running backs and defensive backs up on the line — they called them "hands guys" in football — and having only one kid way back to receive the ball if Sam kicked it deep.

Didn't matter.

The Parkerville Patriots might have suspected an onside kick was coming. What they didn't know was how good Sam was at this, that Sam could have been just as good a soccer player as he was a football player. Didn't know that Sam Brown could make any kind of ball do tricks. He caught the ball just right with the side of his foot, hitting it hard enough to make sure it went the required ten yards, somehow making the ball take one small bounce and then the big one. Just the way he wanted. Making it a kick Ben could run under like it was a pass.

He didn't catch it perfectly in stride, had to dive at the last second to catch it. That was right before what felt like half the Parkerville team fell on top of him, and began trying to rip the ball loose at the bottom of the pile.

They would have had a better chance trying to use their fingers to pull out one of his teeth.

In their league, you kicked the ball off from the forty-yard line. The refs placed the ball at the Parkerville forty-eight. First down, Rams. Kevin Nolti brought in the first play. Quarterback draw. Kevin said, "Coach wanted me to ask you if we're having fun yet?"

Ben said, "Not as much as we're going to have."

He dropped back like he was supposed to, added a little something extra to the play — for fun — a big pump fake like he was going to throw. Froze the up-front defense just enough as he pulled the ball down, ran into the secondary, finally got brought down from the side after gaining thirteen yards.

He looked over at the clock.

Seven minutes left.

Darrelle brought in the next play. Reverse to Sam.

"Love it," Ben said.

Only he got overanxious as Sam ran toward him, wanting Sam to have the ball *right now* and then maybe run all day with it. Ben reached for him too soon, felt the ball coming out of his hands, had to practically bat it through the air to Sam. Too low. It hit Sam just above the knees and dropped to the ground.

Only they got another break, the ball bouncing straight back up into Sam's hands. The timing of the play was way off, but still Sam managed to make a five-yard gain out of it.

"Sorry," Ben said in the huddle, "I nearly blew everything."

"Can't hear a word you're saying," Sam said.

It took them six more plays from there, more plays than Ben wanted, too much time run off the clock. But he'd learned something from the time he started playing sports: The other team wanted to win the game, too. And the Patriots knew they were in a game now. So the Rams ran three plays and Ben threw twice, one an incompletion to a wide-open Justin Bard.

Third and goal from the nine, finally.

The pass was supposed to be a quick slant over the middle to Sam. But he and Justin collided coming off the line, so Ben had to scramble again.

To his left this time.

Still nobody open.

He reversed his field and went back to his right. Flutie time. By now Parkerville had figured out who Ben's go-to guy was, and that the guy was Sam. So they had two guys on him even after the play broke down.

It was why nobody was paying any attention to Kevin Nolti.

Standing by himself in the far left corner of the end zone.

Trying to wave his arms and not draw too much attention to himself at the same time.

Over here.

Ben saw him. In basketball they always said he could see the whole court. Whole football field, too. From where he was near the right sideline, it was a big throw, felt a little bit to him like he was going deep. And his first thought, once the ball was in the air, was that he hadn't put enough on it.

But he had and Kevin barely had to move and now it was 20–14 at The Rock. People always talked about heart in sports, but if they'd never played, they didn't know what it felt like in a moment like this, when you felt your heart wanted to jump right out of you. That's how excited Ben was when he saw the referee on that side of the field put his arms up, signaling touchdown.

Coach crossed up Parkerville on the conversion. It was the same one-step drop as before, just no throw to Sam this time in the corner of the end zone. Ben brought the ball back down, stuck it into Darrelle's belly, Darrelle ran right over the Patriots' middle linebacker to make it 20–16.

Scoreboard said three minutes and three seconds left. Ben wondered if Coach might call for another onside kick. But he didn't. "Kick the sucker deep," Coach said to Sam as he gathered the kick team around him. "We'll stop them and get the ball back. Offense has done its job. Now it's the D's turn."

Grinning at them as he said, "Trust me, I've done this sort of work before."

Ben had looked over at the sidelines a few times during the fourth quarter, just to see if Shawn might have gotten his bad attitude under control, might be cheering them on the way the rest of the guys not in the game were. But he wasn't. As usual he was standing by himself, twenty yards from his closest teammate. It was like he was saying, just with his body language — bad body language to go with his attitude — that if he couldn't be quarterback that he wasn't interested in being part of the team.

Ben thinking one time: What, now he wants to be a quarterback?

Now?

Shawn was so far down the field now he was standing near the Parkerville end zone. But right now Ben didn't have time to worry about him, or his feelings, or trying to sort out the weirdness of it all. Just worried about getting the ball back. Somehow.

It was Coop who finally did that for the Rams.

Coop in there at middle linebacker now. Him in the middle and Ben and Sam behind him at safety. The Core Four guys trying to make it happen, with just over two minutes to play now. Third and six for Parkerville from its thirty-nine. Now the Patriots were the ones who had to make a play, for the first time in the second half. They had been content to sit on the ball and sit on their lead, especially after Coach O'Brien's blitzes had nearly forced Robbie to throw a couple of interceptions early in the third quarter.

But now they had to make a play.

Robbie tried to run for it, knowing that the Rams were out of time-outs, that if he got the first down the game was probably over. And he had blockers in front of him, what looked to Ben like a convoy of them. Blockers and enough room to get to the sticks that meant first down.

Only Coop refused to let it happen. Somehow he broke through the two blockers in front of him, like a door had been opened for him just a crack. Coop broke through the two guys and dove at Robbie's ankles from behind him, got just enough of a piece to bring him down in the backfield.

Two-yard loss.

Fourth and eight.

Parkerville punt.

When Ben ran up to help Coop to his feet, Coop yelled, "I told you we had to play like dogs and then the big dog turns out to be *me*!"

Ben said, "Don't start barking just yet."

"Dude, we got these guys," Coop said.

"Not yet," Ben said.

The Parkerville punter had a good leg, managed to kick the ball away from Ben, out of bounds on the Rams' side of the fifty-yard line. One minute and forty seconds to go.

Fifty-five yards to the end zone.

No time-outs.

Kevin Nolti brought in the first play, the same rollout and short toss to Sam they'd used before. And he brought in another message from Coach O'Brien.

"Coach said he has a confession to make."

"What?"

"Said he really didn't think we had a chance when we were down twenty–zip."

Ben threw it to Sam, who got out of bounds, stopping the clock. Darrelle ran ten yards up the middle. Coach just waved at Ben to call the next play. Ben did, a "Tight End Hook," just a quick buttonhook to Justin for five yards. They were at the Parkerville thirty, clock running, under a minute left now.

Ben called his own number next, a quarterback sweep to the right, knowing he only needed a little daylight to pick up some yards and beat the defense to the sideline.

He did exactly that.

Parkerville twenty-two yard line, fifty seconds left, Rams still down by four.

Now Darrelle brought in the next play. Named for Sam. "Sam Streak" it was called. He was supposed to split out as wide as he could, make a quick fake to the inside, then take off — like a blue streak — down the sideline.

"Goin' for it," Darrelle said.

"Right here, right now," Ben said.

Ben bought himself some time, rolling to his right. The cornerback went for Sam's fake, and after ten yards Sam was in the clear. Ben planted and threw, sure there was no way he could overthrow Sam Brown when he turned on the jets like this.

And sure was wrong.

Wrong, and long. By five yards.

Too excited, too much on it, too far out of Sam's reach. Ben watched the ball fall to the ground. As it did, he slapped the sides of his helmet with both palms. Hard. Feeling in that moment as if he'd blown his best shot to bring his team all the way back.

Sam, of course, acted like it was no big deal. Like he was the calmest guy at The Rock. As usual. "Well, look at the arm on the little guy," he said.

"A big dope actually," Ben said. "I had you."

"Chill," Sam said. "*We . . . got . . . this.*"

They ended up just inside the Parkerville ten, second and goal, twenty seconds left. Coach sent in Kevin with the play. Simply called "Out." Sam was supposed to line up right next to Justin, their tight end, then just run straight for the orange pylon at the goal line, the one that meant touchdown if you got inside it.

Kevin said, "Coach said that if Sam can't get in, or can't get out of bounds, you've still got time to line us up and spike it, we'd still have time for one last play."

"We won't need it," Ben said.

But they did.

The Patriots blitzed this time, all out, and Ben had to rush his throw, which came up short, and low. Sam managed to catch it somehow, but had to come back to the ball to do that, his momentum taking him away from the end zone. The Parkerville guy on him brought him down before Sam could get out of bounds.

Ben had time to look at the scoreboard.

Eleven seconds.

Ten.

He waved the Rams up to the line of scrimmage, yelling "Spike! Spike!" as he did, telling them and the Patriots he was going to spike the ball into the ground, stop the clock, bring up fourth down.

Even as the fire drill was going on, he had time to give a quick look to Sam.

Ben nodded at him.

Sam nodded back.

They both knew what was coming next even if nobody else at The Rock, including Coach O'Brien, did.

Ben wasn't going with a spike.

He was faking one.

It was one of his all-time favorite plays off ESPN Classic, and one of Sam's, they'd watched it plenty of times. Dan Marino against the Jets, faking a spike at the end of a game, coming up and throwing the touchdown pass that won the game for the Dolphins.

Parkerville waited for the spike the way the Jets had that day. Everybody on the field pretty much stopped. Everybody except Ben and Sam, running the play now the way they always had at McBain Field.

What they called "The Full Marino."

Sam was standing all alone at the back of the end zone when Ben threw him the pass that beat the Parkerville Patriots.

The refs didn't even make them bother with a conversion.

Game over.

Rams 22, Patriots 20.

A lot happened next. A lot of running and pounding and Ben ended up at the bottom of another pile, just without the ball this time. Sam still had that. When Ben got loose, Sam was in front of him, handing it to him.

"You know the only one who can make that play?"

"Marino?" Ben said.

"No," Sam Brown said. "A quarterback."

Even Lily was there by the time the Rams had finished shaking hands with the Patriots, waving at Ben from behind the Rams' bench, like she was telling him to get over there right now.

Ben said, "You showed up?"

"Heard big things were happening and hopped on my bike."

"You *heard*?"

Lily said, "It happened like this: Darrelle's sister decided to come watch the game today. Well, actually, her parents *made* her, she didn't really want to. And when the coach put you in at quarterback, she didn't have a cell but Justin's sister did, so she's the one who texted me . . ."

Lily's parents had caved on a cell phone, having originally told her she couldn't get one until she was twelve.

Ben put up both hands, in surrender. "Way too much information," he said. "But I'm glad you came."

"Me, too."

"When did you get here?"

"After your first touchdown."

"So you saw the good parts."

"Did I ever."

"I'm not gonna lie to you, Lils. It didn't stink."

Lily reached across the bench and gave him a high five.

"No, McBain, it definitely did not stink."

He saw Sam and Coop at the other end of the bench, waving at him to get going.

"Hey," Ben said. "We're about to head —"

"Back to your house?"

"Yeah."

"Okay, see you there."

Not asking to come over, just telling. Just being Lily.

"Cool."

"Core Four against the world," Lily said.

"Yeah, girl."

Lily smiled at him now, raising that eyebrow at the same time, like hitting him with both barrels, saying, "What you did today, I *guess* that was the opposite of choking. Right?"

"I guess." Now he smiled at her. "And, Lils? I'm glad you were here."

Lily went to get her bike. Ben turned around and Coach O'Brien was standing there, having waited for Lily to leave, still looking as happy as any of the Rams' players. Like he was eleven.

"I know guys your age never want to hear about the good old days. But, man, I gotta tell you, you took me back today."

"Took you back *where*, Coach?"

"Freshman year at Maryland," he said. "I was the third-string QB, but the starter wasn't getting it done, and the backup was hurt, and we were losing to Wake, and my coach threw me out there when we were down three touchdowns. And I started running around and throwing it around, and we came all the way back." He shook his head, smiling. "Even though *my* coach really didn't think we had a chance that day. Sort of the way I was today."

"I always think there's a chance," Ben said, "long as there's still time."

"I was the exact same way," Coach O'Brien said. "That's why for a while there today, when you were bringing us back, I felt like I was watching *me*."

It was then that Ben saw that Shawn was a few yards away, listening to the whole conversation. When he noticed Ben looking at him, he turned and walked away.

A few minutes later Ben, Sam, and Coop finally walked over to where Ben's parents were waiting for them. But as soon as they got close, Jeff McBain couldn't wait any longer, he stepped up and just bear-hugged Ben.

"You know that NBA commercial on TV?" Ben's dad said. "The one that says the league is where amazing happens? Well, it wasn't hoops today, pal. Amazing was *you*."

"Dad," Ben said, "you're the one who always says you have to play all the way into the parking lot if that's what it takes. So that's what we did."

"Yeah, you did. Now let's say we head across the parking

lot and go home, because your mother is threatening to make what she describes as an epic batch of brownies."

Even on the short ride home, it was as if Ben and Sam and Coop were trying to replay the whole fourth quarter, down by down, all the way to "The Full Marino." They were all still in their football gear, but changing clothes when they got back to Ben's house wasn't a problem, Sam and Coop were always leaving so many clothes behind that Ben's mom just kept a special drawer for them.

Lily showed up about two minutes after the car pulled into the driveway. When she found out Mrs. McBain was making brownies, she said she'd help.

Lily said, "And anybody who says this is girls' work is going down."

Yeah, Ben thought. A good day. No, a *great* day. The guys were all in the basement, waiting for the brownies to be finished, watching Auburn play Florida, when they heard the doorbell. Ben heard his mother yell down for him to get it.

When he opened their front door, Shawn O'Brien was standing there. And as soon as he saw him Ben couldn't help it, he smiled, thinking to himself that now the day was going to end exactly right, Shawn having come over here to make things right between him and Ben.

His way of picking up a teammate, even though the game had been over an hour now.

"Hey," Ben said, "come on downstairs. My mom just made brownies, we're just hanging and watching football."

"I'm not staying," Shawn said.

Staying where he was.

"I just wanted to tell you something myself," he said.

"Dude," Ben said, "it's all good, you don't have to say anything."

"Yeah, I do," Shawn said. "You finally got what you wanted, didn't you?"

"Just a win," Ben said. "It's what we all got."

"No," Shawn said, "you got my *job*."

Ben said. "I was just the QB for one quarter today, that's all."

"C'mon, you know you wanted to be QB from the *first* day."

"No, I didn't."

Ben stopped himself. Ben McBain the bad liar.

"No, that's not true," he said to Shawn. "I *do* love playing quarterback. And, yeah, I'd like to be the starting quarterback. But I like our *team* more. I want our team to do well. That's why I tried to help you. You know I tried to help you. You can't say that I didn't."

Shawn acted as if he hadn't heard the last of what Ben had said. Or if he'd heard, he just didn't care. Ben's mom was always telling him that people were complicated, to never think you had somebody figured out. That there was the person they let you know, and the person they really are. His dad said the same thing about sports stars, especially after Tiger Woods got into trouble and people started to find out about the person he was when he wasn't playing golf. "We know what they do," his dad said, "not who they are."

As Ben stood there, waiting, he decided that Shawn O'Brien was about the most complicated kid he'd ever met. Like there were two Shawns. Or even more than that. All Ben knew about the one standing in front of him was that he was going out of his way to be mean right now. Not here to make the day more right than it already was.

Just trying to ruin it for Ben.

"You've got no idea how sick I am of hearing about you from my dad," Shawn said, his voice rising suddenly, face red. "Sick about hearing what a perfect little teammate you are, what a perfect little player you are. Now he acts like you're his perfect little quarterback. Maybe you should be his son, not me, then everybody would be happy, wouldn't they?"

Shawn grinned then, Ben wasn't sure why, and said, "But there's more than one way to be a perfect son."

Ben didn't know what to say to that, didn't even know where to start, just stood there with his mouth closed, watched as Shawn turned and started to walk back down the front walk.

"Wait," Ben said finally.

Shawn turned around. "I said what I came here to say and now I'm out of here."

Ben said, "Aren't you the same guy who told me you didn't even want to *be* a quarterback?"

Shawn O'Brien shrugged.

"Guess I changed my mind," he said. "Guess I didn't know how much I really wanted to be one until somebody else was.

Perfect little Ben McBain. Seriously, dude? You really *should* be the coach's son."

He got on his bike without turning around again and rode away.

On Monday before practice Coach O'Brien pulled Ben aside and told him that Shawn was still the starting quarterback.

"I just can't do it to Shawn, no matter how much he's been struggling so far," Coach O'Brien said. "I know I'm the coach of the team. But I'm his dad first. Now it's my job as his coach *and* his dad to get the most out of his talent."

"I get that, Coach, I do," Ben said.

"He told me the other night," Coach O'Brien said, "that being the best quarterback he can be is the most important thing in the world to him."

Ben hoped the surprise he was feeling when he heard that one wasn't showing on his face, like some sign that had suddenly been lit up.

This was right before practice, Coach and Ben standing by themselves at the ten-yard line while the other guys stretched.

"Shawn and I had a really good talk when we got home after the game," Coach O'Brien said. "And it nearly broke my heart hearing my own kid telling me how much he wants to get better, not just for me, but for the team."

"Wow," Ben said. Best he could do.

"I know," Coach said.

No, he really didn't know, but it wasn't Ben's place to tell him that.

"Anyway, I did a lot of thinking over the weekend, and came up with what I think is a pretty good compromise to keep Shawn at QB and give you a chance to show your stuff," he said. "What I've done is draw up some of those 'Wildcat' plays they use in the NFL, where the ball is direct-snapped to a back like you and you get to run the offense on that down. And that means run it or pass it. I plan to split out Shawn and have you throw it to him sometimes."

He smacked his hands together, smiling, like he'd just told Ben they were going to a Packers game together.

"Best of both worlds!" Coach said.

Maybe for you, Ben thought.

After everything that had happened, after everything he'd shown once he got his chance, it was as if Coach O'Brien still couldn't see past his own son.

All Ben could hope for in that moment was that the hurt he was feeling didn't show. Nobody ever told him that being a good teammate could hurt this much.

"It's like I'm getting two quarterbacks for the price of one," Coach O'Brien said. "Win-win, right?"

"Right," Ben said.

"I know it's one more position for you to learn, but if anybody can handle it, you can."

Just not the position Ben wanted, the one he knew he deserved, not that he was going to tell Coach that, or even say it that way in front of the rest of the Core Four.

There it was, anyway.

So that's what Shawn had meant when he said there was more than one way to be the perfect son. He had obviously said all the things his dad wanted to hear, obviously pushed all the right buttons with him, to stay the starting quarterback. To get exactly what he wanted.

Ben asked Coach if he had time to make a quick run into school, take a bathroom break. Coach said to go ahead, but hustle back. When Ben got inside, he went running past the boys' locker room, went to the far end of the gym, took his helmet off, and banged it as hard as he could against the padded wall behind the basket, kept doing that as hard as he could until he was ready to go out and act like a good teammate again.

The funny thing was, Shawn could catch a ball a lot better than he could throw one. Everybody knew by now he had a huge problem hitting one of his receivers in the hands. But if *you* hit *him*, it was a different story.

This was one part of football where *he* was money.

Coach had walked them through three or four Wildcat plays before the end of practice, then had the Rams run them. He purposely made them look like a fire drill. The Rams would come out of the huddle looking as if they were about to line up normally. But at the last second, Ben would step back, like he was a quarterback in the shotgun formation, and Shawn would sprint out and line up at wide receiver, usually on the opposite side of the field from Sam.

Sometimes, on "Wildcat Sweep," Ben would just run the ball, behind what felt like a whole lot of blocking. When it was "Wildcat Toss," the play would start out looking like a sweep but then Ben would stop, straighten up, throw to either Sam or Shawn.

When Coach told them the names of the first two Wildcat plays, Coop raised a hand and said, "Whoa there, Coach, this terminology is a little complicated for me."

The rest of the guys laughed.

Coach said, "Cooper, have you always been this funny?"

At the exact same moment, Ben and Sam both shouted, *"No!"*

Ben had to admit, the Wildcat did look like it was going to be fun. On the last play of the night he threw out of the formation when Coach gave him the option to run or throw, hit Shawn between two defenders, Shawn holding on to the ball even as he got hit, as if he went over the middle and made catches like this all the time, no problem.

He didn't acknowledge that Ben had delivered a perfect strike, almost as if the ball had thrown itself, just went over and accepted a high five from his dad before the two of them walked off the field together.

"One big happy family," Coop said. "Or a small one."

"Yeah," Sam said, staring at the O'Briens, "just like our team."

"Hey," Ben said, "if this all *makes* our team better, that's what matters."

"Right," Sam said, "a team that would be a whole lot better off if the plays were starting with you *all* the time."

Coop said, "How come Coach can't see that, 'specially after what you did on Saturday?"

Looking at Ben now.

"Maybe because he doesn't want to," Ben said.

The three of them started walking off the field. Nothing more to say. Ben knew better than they did. Sometimes coaches couldn't see. Past his size. Or past somebody else's size. Whatever. Sometimes they couldn't, sometimes they just plain didn't want to.

But if Wildcat Ben was the best he could do, he'd have to roll with that. And keep his mouth shut about it. If he was going to talk up being a team guy as much as he did, well, he'd better walk the walk, too. That was the deal.

When he got home, he changed into a T-shirt and shorts, finished his homework, walked out to the swings by himself.

It was getting dark on McBain Field, but not too dark, the lights of the houses at this end of the block looking brighter by the minute.

Running the Wildcat for five or six plays a game, the number Coach was talking about, wanting them to use it for the element of surprise, he said, wasn't everything Ben wanted. But at least it was *some*thing. And maybe Coach was right — even if he was dead wrong about Shawn — maybe this was the best of both worlds for the Rams. Now Ben could run the ball some, catch it some, throw it some, all in the same game. If that was going to be his job the rest of the season, if that was his best and only way to help his team get to the championship game, it wasn't as if anybody needed to throw him a pity party.

Ben McBain knew this about himself:

Most of the time he was about as good at feeling sorry for himself as he was being a good loser.

He rocked gently back and forth on the swing. Trying to give himself the kind of pep talk he was sure Lily would be giving him if she were on the swing next to him. Lily never got down about anything, at least not that Ben ever saw or heard. Had as good an attitude about sports and everything else as Ben did.

Maybe that's why the two of them were . . . *Ben and Lily*.

He stayed out there until it was dark, the living room light from the Sheedys' house across from him hitting Ben just right, the way a spotlight would. Ben hopped off the swing then, started running down the middle of the field his buds had named after him. Imagining him running away from the defense the way he had in the fourth quarter on Saturday.

Stopping suddenly as he drew even with his own house, reversing his field, planting his back foot, throwing an imaginary bomb, picturing a perfect spiral flying all the way through the night air, all the way to Sam Brown's house three blocks over.

Like Ben was the one making the Flutie pass to his own best friend. Maybe a pass like it could still happen this season now that he was Wildcat Ben.

Ben stopped now and looked up into the night sky, the way his mom had been making him look up there, at what she called the "big sky," for as long as he could remember, telling him to never look up there without making a wish.

He pictured Sam waiting for the ball to come out of the sky, pressing it to his chest, falling back into the end zone.

Before he crossed the street to his house, Ben wished on *that*.

It was the Friday night before the Kingsland game. Coop's mom was picking them up tonight but was a few minutes late. Coach O'Brien was still on the field behind them, he never left until all the guys on the team had been picked up by their parents. It had been an early practice tonight, and a short one, ending a little after six. Now the Core Four was hanging out in the grass closest to the parking lot, even Lily having shown up to watch some of their practice tonight, her mom having dropped her off.

Lily said she wanted to see this Wildcat thing she'd been hearing so much about with her own eyes.

While they waited for Coop's mom Sam said to Ben, "Ask you something?"

"Sure."

"Why don't we just use the Wildcat *as* our offense?" he said. "Like, our whole offense. Instead of making it just a part of it?"

"Coach likes having both."

"He's wrong about that, like he's wrong about Shawn," Sam said. "Your offense works. Shawn's doesn't."

Now the offense they'd been running all season was Shawn's. Sam didn't make that sound like a good thing.

"It's not his, it's ours," Ben said. "The way the Wildcat is ours."

Ben felt Lily smiling at him before he turned and saw that he was right, she was.

"You know something, McBain?" she said. "You're a good friend even behind people's backs."

"Thanks, Lils," he said. "But I really mean it. It's either all one team or it's not."

"At least you get to be a quarterback some of the time," Sam said. "If you can settle for that, I guess I can, too."

"That's gotta be the deal," Ben said. "If I'm cool with this setup, you guys have to be cool with it. Or that will *not* be cool. With me."

They heard the honk of Mrs. Manley's horn then.

"*Are* we cool?" Ben said, going from one face to another.

"Yeah," Sam said, even though he didn't sound all that happy about it.

Lily put her hand out. The other three put theirs on top of hers.

"Not just cool," Coop said. "Frozen solid."

Ben said, "Solid as ever."

And they were.

The Rams were better than the Kingsland Knights, even on Kingsland's field, better in just about all ways, bigger and faster and, as far as Ben could tell, even better coached.

Better everywhere except on the scoreboard, which said 20–19 for Kingsland with five minutes left in the game.

Shawn hadn't been terrible today, had even managed to complete a ten-yard touchdown pass to Sam for the Rams' first score of the day. But he was still missing too many open receivers: Ben, Sam, Darrelle, Justin. Everybody. Not missing by a lot. But that didn't matter in football.

He was missing by enough.

Ben had gotten to throw four times out of the Wildcat, completing three. It would have been a perfect four for four if Shawn hadn't just cut to the inside when Ben was expecting him to break toward the sidelines, nearly causing an interception.

"I was more open going the other way," Shawn said when he got back to the huddle.

In a low voice Ben said, "Play was to the outside."

"You're such a good QB," Shawn said, "I thought you'd be able to adjust."

Ben couldn't tell whether he was being sarcastic or not, just kept his mouth shut and waited for Kevin Nolti to bring in the next play, Rams at their own forty-two-yard line, needing a score so they didn't fall to 1–3, which Ben was sure would knock them out of any chance of playing for the championship at the end of the season. To him this was the same as a playoff game now, a knockout playoff game, the way every one they played was going to be the rest of the way. Maybe they could get away with another loss. Ben sure didn't think so.

They had to get a score, get the game, get to 2–2, get to Coach O'Brien's fancy bus.

As always for Ben the biggest game was the one he was playing right now. It didn't matter that the Rams should have put this game away long ago, that they should have been two touchdowns better than the Knights, at least.

Get the ball down the field somehow.

On second down Shawn threw high to Kevin coming out of the backfield. Another incompletion, just out of Kevin's reach. Third and ten. Coach crossed up the Knights then, knowing they would be looking for another throw, having Shawn just hand the ball to Ben on a simple off-tackle run. Their right tackle Mike "Moose" Moran threw a huge block, Ben broke it for fifteen yards, nearly broke it all the way.

"Nearly went deep, dude," Coop said, having run down the field to help Ben up. "But we still got plenty of time."

"Winning time," Ben said.

"Any other kind?" Coop said.

There was still plenty of time, so Coach sent in three more running plays, two to Ben, one to Darrelle, all for big gainers, taking them to the Knights' twenty with two minutes left now. Ben wasn't sure if Coach was keeping it on the ground because he was afraid to have Shawn throw. Didn't care. They were moving, he only cared about that. Running the ball, running time, they were going to score and win, he just knew it.

But the Knights made a stand, stopped them twice now. Both times for no gain, Ben once, Kevin once. Third and ten from the twenty. Coach decided to call his last time-out now. Forty-five seconds left. *Here we go again*, Ben thought.

Another one of those games. Maybe the league was that close this season, it was going to be close games like this every Saturday.

Now Coach called for another pass, a simple slant to Sam, Sam just running toward the middle of the field as soon as the ball was snapped, no fakes, no nothing, just run to an empty spot. Shawn wasn't even supposed to drop back, just straighten up as soon as he had the ball in his hands and throw.

He did.

Threw behind Sam.

Badly.

Fourth down. Clock stopped. Forty seconds. One last chance to give themselves a chance to win the game. Winning time. Or not.

Darrelle brought in the play.

A Wildcat play.

Yes! Ben thought.

"Wildcat Option" it was called. The one where he got to decide whether to run or throw. Ben knowing that if he did decide to run, he better be sure he could make it to the sticks, make the ten yards, make the first down. Or the game was pretty much done. And so were they.

In the huddle Shawn said to Darrelle, "You must be joking."

"That's the play your dad sent in," Darrelle said.

"Are you sure?"

"Am I *sure*?" Darrelle looked at Shawn as if he hadn't heard him right.

Shawn nodded at Ben and said, "Maybe you all just want him to be the one to make the hero play."

Darrelle was like Sam. Didn't say much. Said something now. "Are you, like, buggin'?"

Quietly Ben said, "The ref blew his whistle already. We're gonna get a delay of game if we don't run the play."

"You're right," Shawn said, "better call a time-out." He started to put his hands up, make the time-out motion to the ref. Ben grabbed Shawn's arm.

"Don't," Ben said. "We're out of time-outs. We'll get a penalty."

Shawn looked down at Ben's hand on his arm.

Then looked at Ben.

Then did a pretty amazing thing.

He turned and ran off the field.

Ben watched him, wondering how much time was left on the play clock. Maybe Shawn's dad knew he was taking himself out of the game, just like that. But in the moment, he didn't acknowledge that, or hesitate, just shoved Kevin Nolti, standing there next to him on the sideline, out on the field, trying to give him a running start toward the huddle, Kevin going right into a sprint as if he were going out for a pass.

Everything happening at once now.

Ben already had the guys lined up. As Kevin ran past him, Ben said, "Throw me a block," just loud enough for the two of them to hear.

Coop delivered the snap perfectly into Ben's hands, waist high. Ben ran right. Saw Sam up ahead of him, running toward the first-down sticks, making sure he'd be past them if Ben threw him the ball.

Only Ben didn't.

There was too much green in front of Wildcat Ben now. He decided not to take a chance with the ball in the air, as much as he trusted his right arm, trusting his as much as Shawn O'Brien never trusted his own. Decided to run for it.

Oh man, did he know he had to make it.

He ran toward the first-down marker as if that was the finish line in a running race. The guy covering Sam tried to cut back, cut down the angle on Ben. But Sam was running alongside him, and at the last second hit him with a perfect legal block, and sent him flying out of bounds.

When he did, Ben cut back.

Going for it all now. Taking the play straight up the middle of the field, seeing that field open up for him, completely dusting Kingsland's safety, the last guy with any kind of shot at bringing him down.

Ben doing what Coop had just talked about, doing that up as big as he could.

Going deep.

They stayed in the Wildcat for the conversion, same play, same eleven guys on the field, Shawn standing right next to his dad on the sidelines, looking like it was some kind of school detention.

This time Ben pulled up as he ran to his right and threw it to Sam, who'd curled in front of the defensive back covering him, almost like he was a basketball player boxing him out for a rebound. The guy tried to reach over, actually got flagged for interference, but it didn't matter, because Sam held on to the ball. Rams 27, Knights 20. On the second play after the kickoff, the Rams' best cover corner, Tommy Stanley, intercepted a long desperation pass down the field.

Ball game.

Ben made sure his teammates didn't overcelebrate on the field, not wanting to show up the other team. There were just a lot of high fives all around, a few chest bumps, go and get in the handshake line. When the Rams collected again behind their bench, Coach O'Brien walked Shawn over and made him stand in front of the team.

"Go ahead," his dad said.

Coach O'Brien stood there next to his son with his arms crossed. Ben tried to think of a time in his own life when a parent with his arms crossed like that meant anything good was about to happen.

"I want to apologize for leaving the game like I did," Shawn said, staring down at his football shoes the whole time.

Until he looked over at his dad, as if for help.

None coming.

"The rest of it," Coach O'Brien said.

"When you're on a team, you're either in or you're out," Shawn said. "I took myself out today. If you guys let me back in, I promise to do better."

Ben was wondering, listening to the words, listening to the way they came out, if he was just saying them because his dad made him. Or if he really meant them. Ben wondering at the same time if Shawn even knew.

"Go wait at the bus," Coach O'Brien said to Shawn. "I'll let you know what your teammates have to say about this when I get there."

Ben watched as Shawn took another long postgame walk away from the other Rams, away from the game they'd all just played, this walk looking longer to Ben — and much lonelier — than all the others put together.

When he was all the way out of earshot, Coach told them that what Shawn had done, especially with a game on the line, was unacceptable for any player, but particularly for the coach's son. Told them that he'd be perfectly willing to suspend

Shawn if that's what his teammates thought was an appropriate punishment. Told them that he wasn't going to tolerate selfish behavior like that, from his son or from anybody else.

Ben didn't wait for anybody else to speak, pictured himself hitting a hole with the ball under his arm.

"Everybody makes mistakes," he said. "I don't think he needs to miss the next game. My dad says we only get so many of these Saturdays."

"Anybody else?" Coach said.

Ben waited for Coop to say something. But for once, like some kind of miracle, he didn't. Maybe knowing Ben well enough to know Ben didn't want him to.

"Okay, then," Coach said, sounding relieved. "Enough about Shawn. How about we talk instead about the great effort I got out of you guys today. Great, great effort. I wouldn't change one thing about the fourth quarter, other than my kid doing what he did."

He said he'd see them at practice on Monday. The guys went and ripped into the postgame snack that Justin's mom had brought with her from Rockwell. Before Ben could join them, Coach said he had one more thing he wanted to say.

"I should have done this already," Coach O'Brien said. "But you're starting at quarterback next week. You would have started whether I suspended Shawn or not."

Ben took a deep breath. Not wanting to overcelebrate here, either.

"Coach," he said, "I'm totally fine with the way things are now, me in the Wildcat or whatever."

"I believe you are. But I'm not. I may lose my son for a little bit because of this. But if I don't do what's right for the team, if I don't play the best players on merit, than I lose the team."

He started making his own walk toward the bus then. In the distance, the other side of the parking lot, Ben could see Shawn sitting on the steps, waiting for him. Having to know his day wasn't going to get any better, whether he'd escaped getting suspended or not.

Ben watched until Coach got to the bus, watched him and Shawn walk up the steps together, both looking as if they'd lost something important on a day when the Rams had come back to win a big game.

In that moment, Ben McBain felt the same way.

I wanted to be the quarterback of this team more than anything, he told himself.

Just not like this.

No matter how much belief Ben had in himself, and he had a lot, there had always been one big question, through all the times when coaches thought he was too little:

Was he really a quarterback?

If somehow he ever *did* get his chance, the way he was getting it now, could he actually deliver what Coop always called "the goods"?

Turned out he could.

Turned out that when Coach O'Brien did throw him out there, Ben really was the player he'd always imagined he could be.

The Rams had played two games since he had become the starter. They had won easily in the first one, another road game, against Fort Stuart, winning by three touchdowns, Ben throwing for one score to Sam, running for another.

His second start was a much closer game, the Rams only up by six points in the fourth quarter, needing to make some first downs to run out the clock. Ben even completed his first official pass to Shawn, Shawn making a terrific catch between two defenders for the Rams' last first down, the one that really put the game away.

Ben waited until after the game and said to Shawn, "Awesome grab."

Shawn said, "Yeah," then walked away.

It was the longest conversation they'd had since Ben became the starting quarterback.

Ben had thrown for two more touchdowns, the Rams were 4–2 in the league, Ben felt more comfortable being behind center than he had against Fort Stuart, knew he'd feel even more comfortable by next Saturday. But that was the way sports was *supposed* to feel, he thought. The game they'd just played was barely over and already he couldn't wait for the next one. It was like when you saw a great movie and as soon as you got outside the theater you were already thinking about going back to see it again.

Ben felt like that.

"We were more a team today than we have been all season," Coach O'Brien said to them after the handshake line. "If we gave out game balls, I'd want to give one to just about every one of you today, because I felt like everybody in front of me did something to help us win. Shawn? That was a pro catch on the last drive. Great QB-ing from Ben. Sam gets us a pick when it looks like Masters might tie us or go ahead. Blocking, tackling, everything. Two games left. We win them, we're going to the championship game. But we can worry about all that starting Monday night at practice. For now, enjoy the heck out of this one. I don't know what the other coaches were doing today, but what I was doing was looking out there at the best team in our league."

They brought it in around him then and Coach yelled, "Ram tough!" from the TV commercial.

"Ram tough!" they yelled back at him, then went to have their snack.

Ben was one of the last to get in on the snacks. When he turned around, on his way over to where Sam and Coop were sitting in the grass, Shawn was standing there. Most of the time these days, they'd just pass each other without saying a word. But in this moment, Ben thought that was dumb.

So he said, "Your dad was right. That was a pro catch."

"My dad was more interested in the throw," Shawn said, then added, "He's finally got the quarterback he always wanted."

They both knew who "he" was.

About an hour later, after everybody had changed, Ben's dad took Ben and Sam and Coop and Lily into town for ice cream. He said he had to go to the hardware store, then the grocery store to pick up some stuff for dinner, and he'd pick them up at Two Scoops when he was done.

"Now don't celebrate this one *too* much," Jeff McBain said. "Still a lot of season left."

"Don't worry, Mr. M," Coop said. "I'll keep everybody under control."

"Coop," Ben's dad said, "don't take this the wrong way, but I never think of you as being a group leader."

"Ben must get his sense of humor from you," Coop said.

"Nah, his mom. He got his football talent from me."

Ben said, "You got no arm, Dad."

"Well, everything *except* that."

They sat in the back booth and all of them plowed through banana splits and talked about another win, Ben thinking how different everything was now from when they were losing those first two games. It had only taken a few weeks, but now winning felt normal, the way Ben being quarterback did.

So why wasn't he happier?

He knew why.

As badly as Shawn had behaved toward him, and continued to behave — trying to make it sound like Coach O'Brien having the quarterback he always wanted was Ben's fault — Ben still felt badly for *him*. And made the mistake now at Two Scoops of sharing that with the table.

Coop said, "Did you take a helmet-to-helmet shot today I didn't see?"

"C'mon, you got no sympathy for this guy?" Ben said. "For real?"

"For real," Coop said, "and forever."

"You still think you ought to be helping him?" Sam said. "Right. Because of the way he's been such a big help to you."

Then Sam said, "Coop's right."

"Boy," Lily said, obviously trying to lighten the mood, like she did, "you never want to hear yourself saying *that*."

"Go ahead," Coop said, "chirp on me all you want. You can't touch me when I'm eating ice cream."

"Seriously," Ben said, suddenly not hungry, "we don't know what it's like to be this guy. His dad was a QB, he *was* the QB, now he's not. And even though he's making some solid catches and we're winning, maybe he feels like we're doing it without him. Almost like he left the team when he left the huddle that time."

"Dude," Sam said, "when was he ever a *part* of the team?"

Ben wanted to tell them all of it now, about the conversation with Shawn at his house before things started pinballing around in this crazy way, Shawn saying he didn't want to be the quarterback, then saying he did, blaming everything on Ben, catching passes from Ben now instead of trying to throw them to him.

But he couldn't tell. A promise was still a promise, even though keeping it didn't seem all that important anymore.

"I still think there's got to be a way to make him feel like he's a part of the team," Ben said. "And like playing on it the way we do."

"He's not us," Sam said.

"Neither am I sometimes!" Lily said, smiling again.

"Maybe," Ben said, "he just doesn't know *how* to be us."

He heard a knock on the window then, saw his dad, saw Jeff McBain make a goofy face once he knew he'd caught his son's eye. In that moment, Ben thought how it was never hard being Jeff McBain's son, that things never seemed complicated between them, not for one day of Ben's life.

He wondered if Shawn ever felt that way.

To Ben, Coach O'Brien seemed like just as good a guy as Ben's own dad was. But Ben wasn't smart enough to know why that wasn't enough for Shawn.

Maybe, Ben thought, sliding out of the booth, *I'll be able to figure this all out when I'm older.*

Just not today.

Sam and Coop wanted to make the day last even more, said they wanted to see a movie later. Ben said he'd pass, he was just going to stay home and watch college football with his dad, Boston College against Florida State on ESPN. But they all agreed to get a pickup game together tomorrow at McBain Field before the Packers game at four.

It was that time of year now for Ben, either playing football or watching it, all weekend long. Wall to wall.

So Ben and his dad were in the basement at 8:30, a huge bowl of popcorn on the table in front of them. Just the two of them. The football night stretched out in front of them, no school to worry about in the morning, Ben knowing he could stay up until the game ended.

Even better? BC was ahead by a couple of touchdowns early in the second quarter.

During a commercial break Ben's dad said, "Okay, how much does it weigh, I've always wondered?"

Jeff McBain at one end of the couch, Ben at the other.

Ben said, "What does *what* weigh?"

His dad grinned. "Just wondering about the weight of the world. Just how heavy it really is."

"Dad," Ben said, "I've got no clue what you're talking about. I'm fine."

"*Fine?* That's where my guy sets the bar after a big win like today? You're just fine?"

"A little tired, maybe."

"Talk to me, big boy."

"About being tired?"

"About whatever it is that's bothering you, because something *is*."

Ben's dad pointed the remote, muted the set. The basement was quiet now.

"I'm fine, really."

"You should be," Jeff McBain said, "but you're not."

Ben took a deep breath, let it out, the sound way louder than normal because of the sudden quiet in the room.

"I see how some of the other dads are sometimes, how out of control they can get about sports," Ben said. "But you never put any pressure on me."

"Mostly because these games are important enough to you already."

"But I know how much you want me to do well."

"In the worst way, kiddo. Which is a good thing for parents and a bad thing, all at the same time. Because you're right, you see and hear the same stuff I do, sometimes we do want things for our kids in the worst way. And I do mean the *worst* way. I do see it at your games all the time, all around me in the stands. It's why I try to cheer as quietly as possible. I figured out a long time ago that *your* games aren't about *me*."

Ben could see the players back on the field on the big screen. His dad kept the sound off.

Jeff McBain said, "But I have the feeling this isn't about you. Or us."

"No, Dad, we're cool. Totally."

"Cool."

"I never asked you this before," Ben said, "but when you were my age, you ever feel any pressure from Grandpa?"

The force of his dad's laugh surprised Ben.

"All the time!" he said.

"But Grandpa is, like, the nicest man in the world."

"A living saint," Ben's dad said about his own. "Still doesn't mean it can't get tricky between a father and a son, no matter how much they love each other. That's the way it was with your grandfather and me and baseball."

"But football was your favorite."

"Let me finish," his dad said. "Football *was* my favorite. But baseball was Grandpa's. So he wanted it to be mine, too. He wanted me to be a pitcher the way he was, even though as you've pointed out, I don't have much of an arm. So I did try to pitch. For him." He smiled. "But I couldn't pitch the way he had."

Ben turned so he was facing his dad now, listening up good. He had never heard this one. His dad had told a lot about what it was like when he was a boy. Never this.

"But I knew I didn't have it. In my heart of hearts, I knew something else: I didn't have it in me to love baseball. It was just something I did with my buddies in the spring. And even though Grandpa never said a word, I knew *he* knew, and that it just killed him. He was a baseball guy, it was the only sport that mattered when he was growing up. Not just the national pastime. *His*. Oh, he'd go and watch me play football — which I really do love the way you do — but his heart wasn't in it. And as sad as I just knew it made him, it made me even sadder."

Ben said, "You two ever talk about it?"

Jeff McBain laughed again, not as loud as before, though. "Talk about *stuff*? With my *dad*? I grew up before that was popular."

"We talk all the time."

"Well, your grandpa and I didn't."

"He talks about stuff with me."

"He's gotten much better at it the second time around."

"Do you wish you'd talked it out, about you and him and baseball?"

"Constantly," Ben's dad said. He un-muted the television now, almost like he was bringing this talk between them to an end. "There's a part of me, even now, that wonders how much of it he could see, and how much he just didn't want to. Like he kept thinking I would eventually come around."

Jeff McBain said, "Any of this making any sense to you?"

"A lot."

"Wait a second! Weren't we supposed to be talking about what was on your mind?"

Ben smiled now at his dad, a smile that felt as if it came all the way up out of *his* heart of hearts.

"Actually, Dad, we did."

When the game was over, when Ben was up in bed with his lights out, he thought about everything his dad had said to him in the basement.

All his life, at least until Coach O'Brien put him in at quarterback, Ben thought it was only him that coaches couldn't see. Couldn't see the player he was supposed to be. Couldn't see him for what he really was.

But maybe he wasn't alone.

If it had happened to his dad, maybe it happened to everybody.

Right before Ben went to sleep, he came up with his plan.

Two home games left in the regular season, one against Darby that coming Saturday, one against Glendale the next.

Parkerville and Glendale were tied for first place, both with 5–1 records. Rockwell and Darby were 4–2. If the Rams won out, they'd not only end up 6–2, they'd have beaten the other three teams fighting to get into the championship game.

Math wasn't always Ben McBain's best subject, but the football math here was pretty simple:

Win two games and nobody could keep them *out* of the championship game, no matter what anybody else did. Even after their 0–2 start, even after everything that had happened with Shawn, if they kept winning now — as Ben just knew they would — they would win the league.

He wasn't saying that out loud, of course.

Not because he was superstitious or afraid of jinxing the Rams. Just because he knew you were never *ever* supposed to get ahead of yourself in sports. You started thinking about anything except the game you were playing and then the math got *real* simple:

The other team would score more points and you'd lose.

The Rams had fought too hard, fought *back* too hard, to allow that to happen now.

"This feels like our version of the Turkey Bowl," Coop said when they were warming up on the field before the Darby game, the weather much cooler all of a sudden, the first time all year it had felt like real football weather.

Darby and Rockwell were big rivals in everything, Darby being the next town over. Every year, no matter what the records were for Rockwell High and Darby High, the Turkey Bowl game on Thanksgiving felt like the championship of the two towns.

Sam said, "Just try not to play like a turkey today."

Coop said, "How come you never talk to him like that?"

Pointing at Ben.

"Because he never acts like a turkey."

"And I do?" Coop said.

Sam grinned. "Gobble, gobble," he said.

"You know," Coop said, "for all this Core Four stuff, it sure seems like only *one* of us is the one always getting his chops busted."

"We just think that the best way to get you up for the game is to knock you down a little bit," Ben said.

"Thanks for caring," Coop said. "And sharing."

They all knew a lot of the Darby guys from other sports, knew their best player was their halfback Ryan Hurley, knew the Darby Bears were going to run Ryan all game long, that their coach didn't like to throw. Nobody in the Midget Division was going to take time to scout another team, not even some-one who loved to be prepared the way Coach O'Brien did. But he told them in his pregame talk that maybe he *had* talked to a couple of the coaches whose teams had played Darby already, so he pretty much knew what to expect.

"Smash-mouth football all the way," he said. "But let them go ahead and try to run over this team." Nodding as he said, "When we've got the ball? We run over *them*, and around them, and past them. And throw over them."

By the time the first half was nearly over, Ben wished it were that simple. Because for the first time since he'd become quarterback, the offense wasn't clicking. The best scoring drive of the day had belonged to the Bears, their first drive of the way, Ryan Hurley getting the ball on practically every down. They ended up with a first and goal from the Rams' five, but when it looked like Ryan was about to run it in for the game's first touchdown, Coop closed the ground between them, rocked him with a hit from the side that knocked the ball loose, recovered it himself.

"Gobble, gobble," Coop said to Ben and Sam in the hud-dle. "Who's a turkey now?"

The Rams ran it out of there for a couple of first downs. But Ben was missing with his throws today, long and short. A couple had been batted down by the big guys in the Bears' front line. The Rams' best chance to score came right at the end of the half, but then Ben tried to force in a pass to Sam, who was double-covered the way he had been all day — obviously Coach O'Brien wasn't the only one who had done a little scouting — and got picked off by Ryan Hurley, back playing safety.

So the game stayed 0–0.

Ben didn't know what his passing stats were exactly, he was too busy playing the game. But he could only remember three completed passes for the half, two to Sam, one to Shawn. The rest of the time he really had been about as accurate as Shawn had been when he was still the starting quarterback for the Rams.

He had come to The Rock with his big plan today. Scrapped now. In the wind. The only plan was to somehow find a way to win the game.

"Don't worry," Sam said to him when they got to the bench. "I'll figure out a way to get open."

"Yeah, well if you do, maybe I can start remembering how to get the ball to you," Ben said.

"You will."

"And you know this . . . *how?*"

"Because you always have," Sam said. "It's nothing–nothing. So it's like we're starting the game all over again."

But it stayed nothing–nothing into the fourth quarter. Tie game, biggest crowd of the season because it was Darby, another Saturday that felt like a playoff game because of what was at stake, the game almost feeling like sudden death, because you just knew that the first team to score was going to win. The Rams had played all those other close games, Ben knew, but this one was more of a grind, like they'd been playing uphill on offense from the start.

He knew something else: A tie might be as bad as a loss, especially if Glendale won *its* game against Parkerville today and got to 6–1. Because then even if the Rams beat Glendale next weekend, Glendale would finish 6–2 and the Rams would finish 5–2–1.

And if Parkerville won *its* last game, the Rams were out of the championship.

Rams ball on their own thirty, three minutes to go.

Finally Ben got them moving again. No smash-mouth football for the Rams now. Coach O'Brien had them throwing on every down. "Remember when the Mavs won the championship from LeBron last year?" Coach had said to Ben before the drive. "Dirk Nowitzki missed eleven of his first twelve shots. And you know what he did? He kept shooting. Well, we're going to do the same, because I just know you're about to get hot."

First down pass to Sam. Then another. They were at midfield, just like that. Short pass to Darrelle out of the backfield. Then another to Darrelle. Inside the Bears' forty. The Bears were still doubling Sam, but Ben *was* hot now, put one between the two defenders and the Rams had a first down on the Bears' twenty.

Clock running, inside a minute.

Kevin Nolti brought in the play from Coach O'Brien: "Lookaway" it was called. Ben liked it. He was supposed to fake a throw to Sam on the right, then look the other way and hit Shawn on the left sideline, ten yards or so past the line of scrimmage. They ran the play a lot in practice in two-minute drills. Shawn knew he was supposed to step out of bounds after the catch, stopping the clock.

"We got this," Ben said in the huddle. He was talking to all of them, but looking at Shawn. Like he was trying to make him believe he could make this catch.

As they broke the huddle, Shawn O'Brien said the first words he'd said to Ben all day.

"I know the play's to me," he said. "But if Sam's open, throw it to him. *Please*." Not the Bad Shawn now. *Or* even close. Just a scared kid.

"No," Ben said. "Like I said, we got this."

Thinking to himself that sometimes things worked out the way they were supposed to, you didn't need a plan, you just had to let it happen.

He dropped back into the shotgun. Coop gave him a perfect snap, waist high. Ben sold the fake to Sam as hard as he could, Sam double-covered again. For one real bad moment, Ben was afraid he'd sold the fake too well, felt the ball slipping out of his hand as he brought his arm forward.

He managed to hold on. And it was as if the whole defense had leaned in Sam's direction when Ben made his fake. So when he did look to the left, Shawn was wide open, having stopped just as a way of not drawing any attention to himself, as if he were as surprised as anybody at how open he really was.

Ben hoped that Shawn knew how much open *field* there was in front of him, that he didn't need to go out of bounds, that he could take this sucker all the way once he had it in his hands.

Take it all the way to the house.

Ben threw a tight spiral to him, as good a pass as he'd thrown all day, the ball feeling just right coming out of his right hand. It came at Shawn like a perfect strike in baseball, down the middle of the plate. He wore "11," like his dad had before him.

If he'd taken his hands out of the way, the ball would have hit him right between the ones.

Shawn dropped it.

Maybe he'd taken his eyes off it just for a split second, having seen what Ben saw, all that open field in front of him. Knowing all he had to do was catch it and run. But he didn't. He dropped it the way Ben had earlier in the season, when Shawn was the one doing the throwing.

Shawn ended up staring at the ball on the ground in front of him like some bottle he'd just dropped and smashed all over the kitchen floor.

He finally jogged back to the huddle, head down.

"Don't worry about it," Ben said. "It was only first down."

In a voice Ben could barely hear, Shawn said, "Don't try to make me feel better."

Nothing more to say, because Darrelle brought in the next play then. Another simple name for it: "Post." Sam over the middle. Another one where he was just supposed to get his shoulder inside the corner covering him and make one of his quick cuts over the middle. As much of a money play as they had.

Until Ben changed it.

In the huddle he said, "We're gonna run Lookaway again."

In a voice almost as quiet as Shawn's had been, Sam Brown said, "You're calling an *audible*? *Now*?"

Coop said, "Dude. You haven't called an audible all year."

"They won't be expecting it," Ben said.

"You mean, because we aren't, either?" Coop said.

Shawn acted as if he wasn't listening to the others, just looked at Ben now and said, "Why are you doing this?"

"Because it gives us our best chance to win the game," Ben said.

"My dad knows better," Shawn said.

Ben said, "Not everything."

Ben told Sam he could even yell for the ball this time. To Shawn he said, "Don't stop running until you get to the end zone. That's where the ball will be."

"I *can't*."

"Run or catch?" Ben said. "You can do both."

Before Coop walked up and bent over the ball he said to Ben, "You *do* know what you're doing, right?"

"Trust me."

"Always have, always will."

Sam was actually a yard behind the coverage when he yelled for the ball. Ben almost threw it to him. Didn't. Sold his fake again, turned, and picked up Shawn, sprinting down the sideline. Only this time the kid covering him hadn't bit on the fake, was running almost shoulder to shoulder with him.

Trust it, Ben told himself.

Trust yourself and trust him.

He thought he'd led Shawn just right, until he saw at the last second that he'd put the ball too far out in front of him.

But then he saw something else, the way everybody at The Rock and everybody from the two towns did. Saw Shawn O'Brien laying out as far as he could, like he was doing a racing dive off the side of a swimming pool. Saw him stretching out his arms and his big hands as he hit the ground hard, bouncing a couple of times before he showed the ref that he'd held on.

The ref puts his own arms and hands up and signaled touchdown.

And in that moment, Shawn became a Ram.

Not a *scared* kid now. Just a big, happy one. He jumped up and handed the ball to the ref and then put his arms in the air, pumping them up and down as he sprinted for his teammates.

Like he really was one of them now.

"What the heck?" Ben heard Coop say. "What the heck?" And ran straight for Shawn, the two of them launching each other into a crazed, flying chest bump.

For this one moment, Shawn O'Brien looked happy. Or maybe, Ben thought, he just looked like a football player.

At last.

Shawn didn't celebrate with Ben, didn't say anything to Ben until the game was over, until Ben had run around left end for the conversion that made the final score 8–0, Rams. Until Sam, playing the deepest safety he'd ever played, had intercepted a long pass intended for Ryan Hurley on the last play of the game.

Then Shawn came walking over to where Ben stood at midfield.

Ben could see how awkward this was for him, knew at the same time there was nothing he could do to make it any easier for him.

Shawn put out a fist, Ben bumped it, Shawn said, "I owe you one."

Ben could see he surprised him when he came back with, "Yeah, you do."

"Well, go ahead and name it," Shawn said.

"I want *you* to make *me* a promise," Ben said.

"I can't," Shawn said.

This was at McBain Field, an hour after the game had ended, Ben having waited to tell Shawn what he wanted.

"You ever notice how much you say that?" Ben said. "That you can't do something?"

"Just let me wait until the season's over," Shawn said.

Ben said, "Man, there really is a ton of stuff you just don't get. The season's just getting *started*, that's the way I look at it. And the way *you* ought to be looking at it."

It was just the two of them, far end of the field near the swings, Shawn having ridden his bike over, Ben having laid it all out for him, like a homework assignment:

Shawn had to tell his dad all of it. Now. That he didn't want to be a quarterback, never wanted to be a quarterback, didn't want to be the player his dad had been.

"I'd have to admit I lied," Shawn said. "My dad hates lying."

"You think mine doesn't?" Ben said. "But the longer you let the lie go on, the worse it's going to be when you do tell. Like any dumb lie. That's why you're gonna do it now."

They were sitting in the grass near the swings. Shawn had told Ben he wasn't going to sit in some little kid's swing, Ben wanting to tell him he ought to try it, he did some of his very best thinking sitting in those swings.

For now they were in the grass instead, facing each other, Shawn wearing a "Maryland Football" T-shirt. His dad's old school.

"The day he put you in at quarterback, that was the day I told him I was going to try harder than ever to *be* one. A QB."

"Another lie."

"I *know*."

"After you caught the touchdown pass today, you said you owed me one, all I had to do was name it. This is the one."

Shawn said, "I didn't know what you wanted me to promise."

"Tough," Ben said, grinning at him as he did. "It's like you've been telling me. A promise is a promise. You gotta go home and tell your dad the player you were today — *that's* the player you're supposed to be."

"You're sure about that because I caught one touchdown pass?"

"Totally!" Ben said. "Seriously, dude, how dense can you be? Everybody saw."

"I'm *gonna* tell my dad, you do have my word on that. Just let me wait. If we win two more games, we win the championship, he'll be happy, I'll be happy, everybody will be happy. It will be easier then."

"Who said anything about easy?" Ben said. Shook his head. "Nope. Do it today."

Shawn started to say something, but Ben held up a hand. "If you don't tell him, I will."

"You can't," Shawn said. "You *did* promise."

"Yeah," Ben said, "I did. But I've been thinkin' on that one. And here's what I came up with: Before I made that promise to you, I made the same promise to my*self* I make before every season."

"Which is?"

"To be the best teammate I can possibly be. Which is what I'm trying to be now with you."

"By making me do something I don't want to do?"

"No," Ben said. "By getting you to get over yourself." Grinning at him again.

Shawn said, "I've been trying to tell you something all season: I'm not like you. I want to be more like you, I think that's why I came to you in the first place, as messed up as I acted after, even though it killed me to admit that to myself. But I'm *not* . . . like . . . you."

Ben said, "But, see, that's how this thing did get messed up. And that's as much my fault as yours. You're not *supposed* to be me. Or Sam. Or Coop. They tell me all the time that you're not like us. Well, guess what, dude? You're not! You gotta be the player you want to be. Not the one your dad wants you to be. Because that would be *really* messed up."

Shawn just studied him, listening, as Ben said, "I know you better than I used to, but I'm not gonna say I know you that well. But even I know you've been playing for him and not for you."

"My dad never *asked* me to do it for him."

Ben could hear his own dad's voice inside his head now, talking about Ben's grandfather and baseball and pitching and all the rest of it.

He said, "Sometimes dads don't have to ask."

Now Shawn got up, walked over to one of the swings, sat down in it, pushed off, rocked back and forth for a minute. When he stopped he said, "After the season."

Ben shook his head again.

Shawn said, "You always get what you want?"

Ben laughed. "Heck, no," he said. "You might have noticed, sometimes I have to wait for stuff."

Shawn hopped off the swing now.

"I'm gonna head," he said.

"Okay."

"I'm still not promising anything," he said.

Ben reminded him for the last time that he already had.

He didn't hear from Shawn Saturday night. No messages from him when he got back from church on Sunday morning, on the answering machine or on e-mail.

Now it was early Sunday afternoon, the Clayton brothers on their way over to McBain Field for the touch football game they'd planned. Sam and Coop were already at Ben's house, on the back porch, drinking lemonade, hanging. Lily was with them, even threatening to play today, the rest of the Core Four knowing she could more than hold her own with the guys, she was that good and that fast.

Not one of them ever daring to add, *For a girl.*

Ben had filled them in on his conversation with Shawn the night before, telling them as much as he could without telling everything. Lily, as always, was the one listening closest.

"Let me understand you," she said. "You're *making* him tell his dad he wants to be a receiver? Why does that matter to you so much?"

"Makes us a better team," he said. "His dad probably feels bad that he had to move Shawn off quarterback. And I'm thinking Shawn feels bad because his dad feels bad."

"Really," Lily said.

"Lils," Ben said, "you didn't see the catch he made yesterday."

"So you've got it in your head that if everybody is happy at his house, this will make him an even better receiver somehow?"

Staying with him. Like she was covering him in a game.

"Pretty much," Ben said.

"I still don't get why it's such a big deal," Lily said.

"I'm kind of clueless, too," Coop said.

"There's a shocker," Sam said.

"Can I take one more shot at explaining this?" Ben said.

Coop said, "Quiet, everybody. McBain speaks."

"Shawn has spent the whole year getting in his own way," Ben said.

"And yours," Sam said.

"Whatever," Ben said. "Now I'm thinking that if he can get *out* of his own way, he won't just be a good player, he could even be, like, *great.*"

Lily said, "Off one catch."

Ben said, "Listen, I'm not smart enough to figure this all out —"

"Liar," Lily said. But smiling as she did.

"— but I think getting it out in the open that he's doing what he likes to do instead of what he thinks he *has* to do for his dad, it will make him better and us better and end of story, I'm tired of talking about this now."

"All about the team," Lily said.

"Basically."

Lily smiled again. "Liar," she said again.

"Why do I have to be lying?" Ben said. "You know how much I want to win. In everything."

Coop jumped in now, saying, "It sounds like Ben is saying that if Shawn just chills with his dad, he'll have more fun, and having more fun will make him a better player. Am I right?"

"Exactly!" Ben said. "Look at the Coop man, explaining it better than I did."

"I did?" Coop said.

They ended up playing three-on-three, Lily even scoring a couple of touchdowns for Ben's team, a fun game finishing about
three o'clock. Still plenty of time before the Packers played.
Sam and Coop said they were going to ride their bikes into
town to get ice cream, they'd be back before the kickoff. Lily
left for soccer practice.

Ben thought about just calling Shawn for an update,
decided instead to do what he'd done the last time, get on his
bike and take a ride over there. Just show up. It was a Sunday
in the fall, Shawn's dad had played in the NFL, they had to be
home watching football, probably the Colts game Ben knew
had started at one.

Ben told his dad where he was going.

"So things are better between Shawn and you?" Jeff
McBain said.

"Sort of why I'm going over there," Ben said. "To find out."

When Ben got to Shawn's house, he pushed the intercom
button, waited until he heard Mrs. O'Brien's voice, told her it
was Ben McBain to see Shawn.

Mrs. O'Brien said, "Hey, Ben. Shawn and his dad are back on the field. They have been for a while. I'm up to my elbows making lasagna, you can find your own way back, right?"

He said he could as the gate opened.

This time he made it all the way up the driveway without getting off his bike, like doing that was some kind of challenge for him. Like one more hill for him to climb today. When he got to the top, he left the bike leaning against their front porch, went around the big house and back to where the cool turf field was.

When he got close, he stopped near a big old tree, just so he could see Shawn and his dad before they saw him.

And then Ben had his answer.

There was his answer as plain as day on the field below him, without Shawn or his dad having to say a single word, to Ben or anybody else.

Ben didn't see Mr. O'Brien trying to be Shawn's quarterback coach. Or even trying to be the coach of his team today. Just being Shawn's dad.

Not showing Shawn how to grip a ball today or throw one. Throwing the ball *to* him instead. Both of them looking as if they didn't want to be anywhere else in the world. Like the two of them were finally where *they* were supposed to be.

Watching them now, Ben thought of the times at practice when he'd sneak a look at Coach O'Brien, back when Shawn was still the quarterback and would make a good throw. And Ben would see Coach smiling.

He was smiling like that today. The only difference was that Shawn was finally smiling back.

Ben stayed behind the tree, poking his head around the trunk enough to see Shawn's dad throwing long. And short. Making Shawn dive sometimes. Making him jump. No mechanical receiver on the field today. No need for Chad Ochocinco on Wheels.

Just Shawn O'Brien.

One time Coach threw a ball to Shawn on a post pattern and even though Shawn caught it, his dad yelled, "Is that your idea of a *sharp* cut?"

Shawn yelled back, "I caught it, didn't I, old man?"

They both laughed.

Ben stayed behind the tree a long time, stayed until he figured he had to be getting close to the start of the Packers' game. Waited until Coach O'Brien dropped back and threw one more deep ball, Shawn running under it and catching it in stride.

Then Ben made a clean getaway.

He made his way back up the hill toward the house, taking his time, still hearing shouts from behind him, and cheers, and more laughter.

Ben thinking to himself that this was the way all sports were supposed to sound, not just football.

He was on his laptop later, watching Flutie, telling himself he didn't have to wait until the season was over, he was a quarterback now.

Not the Flutie who played with his dad at Boston College, the little big man who threw the Hail Flutie pass that time against Miami. No, tonight Ben was watching highlights from when Doug Flutie played in the Canadian Football League, when he was one of the greatest players in the whole history of that league.

Ben loved watching Flutie's old CFL highlights on YouTube even now:

Twelve guys to a side, everybody allowed to be in motion before the ball was snapped, the end zones twenty yards deep, the field 110 yards long and wider than the regulation fields for American football.

It was like watching a football video game, just with real players. All that room for Flutie to make things up as he went along. All that pure fun for him, even if he had only gone up there to play — Ben knew from his dad — because he got tired of the NFL telling him he was too small to play quarterback. This was way before he came back later with the Buffalo Bills and proved everybody wrong by taking the Bills to the playoffs one year, before a dumb coach put him back on the bench and the Bills lost to the Tennessee Titans.

One more dumb coach, Ben knew by now, who couldn't see the quarterback Flutie was born to be.

Here was Ben up in his room, loving on Flutie's CFL highlights, when his mom poked her head in and told him that he had a visitor.

"Your coach," she said.

Coach O'Brien was at the bottom of the stairs, talking to Ben's dad.

"I kept hearing about McBain Field from Shawn," he said. "Checked it out when I got out of the car. Pretty cool."

"Not as cool as your field," Ben said.

"From what I hear about what goes on with you and your buddies over there across the street," he said, "I wouldn't be so sure about that."

Then to Ben's parents he said, "Can I borrow your boy for just a minute?"

Beth McBain said, "You can. But we're going to have to insist that you return him."

Coach and Ben went outside, sat down on the top step of the front porch.

"Thank you," Coach said to Ben.

"Coach," he said, "you don't have to thank me for anything."

"Actually, I do," he said, "now that Shawn told me *every-thing.*" He put his head down, gave it a quick shake, said, "Everything I should have been able to figure out on my own."

"It's all good," Ben said.

"Now it is," Coach said. "Thanks to you."

Adding: "I couldn't see what my boy wanted because of what I wanted for him."

"No worries," Ben said. "He's gonna be great now, wait and see."

"I don't know about that," Coach said. "But what I do know is that he's gonna have a great time trying."

He turned and put out his hand and Ben shook it, making sure to look Coach in the eyes as he did, the way his parents had taught him.

"You called that audible on purpose," Coach said, "didn't you?"

"I did," Ben said.

"To open my eyes."

Ben said, "Maybe open everybody's."

"I didn't see him, I didn't see *you*," Coach O'Brien said. "Some coach."

Ben smiled at him. "Don't beat yourself up," he said. "Being a grown-up is *hard* sometimes."

"Tell me about it."

Now Coach O'Brien stood up, walked down the steps, turned around.

"Even before I put you behind center," he said, "I thought you were one of those guys who could really see the field. I just didn't know how much until now."

Ben stood up now on the top step, looking down at his coach for once.

"If you don't keep your eyes open," Ben said, "you might miss somebody finally breaking into the clear."

Championship Saturday at The Rock.

Parkerville had ended up with the best record, its only loss to the Rams, and normally would have had home-field for the championship game. But the Patriots played their home games on the town's high school field, and the high school team needed it, so the big game had been bumped over to the Rams.

Robbie Burnett and his guys had stomped Kingsland in their last regular-season game. The Rams had beaten Glendale by two touchdowns in *their* last game, breaking a tie in the fourth quarter, both of the scores coming on passes, one from Ben to Sam, the other to Shawn.

So here they were.

Here they were having won out after being 0–2, here they were coming into the big game feeling like they were the best team in the league even if the team they were playing had the best record and had Robbie Burnett, whom everybody thought would be the best quarterback in the league coming into the season.

Just not according to Cooper Manley.

"We've got the edge at QB, most definitely," Coop was saying on the walk from the parking lot to the field with Ben and Sam, the three of them the first to arrive, as usual.

"You sure about that?" Ben said.

"*So* sure," Coop said. "He's bigger, you're better."

"*We're* better," Sam said. "About to prove it."

Man of few words, as always.

They started to warm up, soft-tossing with Ben's ball, Ben having brought the ball from home for good luck today. A few minutes later Coach O'Brien and Shawn arrived, Shawn running out on the field to join them, as if that was the most natural thing in the world now.

The four of them tossed Ben's ball around and, when they were done, went over and sat down on the bench.

Shawn said to Ben, "I've been feeling pressure like you can't believe since I woke up this morning. Like, woke up as early as if it were a *school* morning. Without my parents yelling at me to get up."

"Dude," Ben said, "this isn't pressure today. This is like finally getting to the good parts of the movie."

Coop said, "*Seriously?* Pressure was when you hated on football and we hated on you."

There was no hesitation: Shawn laughed along with everybody else. Ben decided that if he was faking it, it was the best fake he'd made all year in football.

Sam said to Shawn, "Sometimes Coop manages to make sense. It's like that one you always hear from your parents, about the blind squirrel occasionally finding the acorn."

"I'm in too good a mood for you to hurt my feelings," Coop said. "So there's no point in even trying."

Ben said to Shawn, "Listen, everybody's feeling *some* pressure today. But it's the good kind, when you're, like, stupidly excited about something."

Ben McBain *was* stupidly excited.

Had been all morning. Waiting to leave for the field once *he* woke up early. Waiting for the game to start now. Watching as people, from both towns, started to fill up the stands. He was excited even watching Robbie Burnett and the rest of the guys from Parkerville warming up at the other end of the field now that their bus had arrived.

His dad really was always telling him that he was only going to get so many Saturdays like this in his life, so he better appreciate them. Ben thought: *I've been appreciating this one all day, let's play the game.* Now.

Finally it was five minutes to one and Coach O'Brien was gathering them around him, about ten yards onto the field.

"Gonna keep it simple today," he said. "I can see, just looking at you, how ready you all are. I know because I've been there, had my own share of big-game days like this in my own life. For some of you, this is the first time you've had a game like this that feels like a Super Bowl. But I'm gonna say the same thing to you as I'm saying to everybody: Enjoy every minute of it today. And know this from your old coach: I'd much rather be playing this one than coaching it."

He put his hand out in front of him. The guys crowded in, put their hands with it.

"Ram tough!" Coach O'Brien shouted.

The Rams shouted back even louder.

Big game, big day, no more waiting, let's do this.

When they pulled away from Coach, Ben said to Sam Brown, "You ready?"

"You know it."

Then Sam said, "By the way? You *are* better than Robbie Burnett."

The Rams scored the first two times they had the ball.

The Patriots scored the first two times *they* had the ball.

It was going to be one of those games, like both offenses planned to be on the fast break all day long, running up and down the field like there was some kind of shot clock on them.

At one point, Ben and Sam both back at safety, both of them unable to stop Robbie Burnett from completing one pass after another, Sam said, "Didn't we cover these guys the last time we played them?"

"It seems like there's more of them this time," Ben said. "Like they've got us outnumbered, even though it's eleven on eleven."

"Good news?" Sam said. "The guys on their defense feel the exact same way."

But Robbie just kept spreading his passes around. Wideouts, tight ends, running backs. Doing it like a pro. Like he really did think *he* was the best quarterback in the Midget

Division. No way to guess where he was going to go next. And just when they thought they knew where he *was* going next, he'd pull the ball down and run.

The good news for the Rams was Ben was playing the same game, running with the ball even more than Robbie was, keeping the Patriots' defenders off balance every time he'd roll out again, their guys unable to get a solid read on whether he was running or passing.

A good thing, for the Rams, anyway.

With two minutes left in the half, Coach sent in a play that gave Ben the option to run or throw to Sam on a third and six. But as soon as Ben got outside the pocket, he saw enough room for him to keep the ball and make the first down himself. One pretty awesome head fake later — Ben had to admit to himself — and one equally awesome cutback in the open field, he had run forty yards for a touchdown. Then threw it to Sam over the middle for the two-point conversion.

Rams, 21–13.

"Let's see Robbie Burnett bust a move like that," Coop said.

"Let's just get a stop," Ben said.

They didn't. They had their chance, had the Patriots at fourth and two at the Rams' nineteen with thirty seconds left in the half, packed the line sure that Robbie would run the ball, especially since he still had two time-outs left. Only then Robbie executed an all-world fake — "all galaxy," as Coop called it after the play — to his fullback, straightened up, and threw a perfect pass to his tight end, who'd run right past Ben and Sam.

On the conversion, Robbie *did* hand it to his fullback, who ran up the middle and right through Cooper Manley and into the end zone with the two points that made it 21–21 at halftime.

Ben and Sam walked over to where Coop was still on the ground, each put down a hand to lift him up.

Coop said, "You know what I *really* hate? When the other team really does want to win as much as we do."

"No," Ben said to him, "they don't."

After they'd all gotten drinks, Coach O'Brien told them something they all knew already: They needed stops if they were going to win themselves a championship today.

"I did a lot of subbing on defense, as you guys probably noticed," he said, grinning as he added, "Not that it helped out a whole heck of a lot. But I did it because I want everybody fresh the rest of the game. Anybody who thinks he needs a blow for a play or two, don't try to be a hero, let me know. Because one tired play could be the difference between winning or losing."

He got down on one knee then, looked up at them.

"The team I believe you guys are?" he said. "Go out there and be that team now."

Before they took the field, Coach grabbed Ben by the arm and said, "And you be the quarterback you always believed *you* were."

But on the fourth play of the second half, the Rams having driven the ball over midfield again, Ben threw a little hook pass to Shawn on the left side, about five yards past the line of scrimmage, a nice safe play on third and three.

Only when Shawn turned it upfield, he saw he had some room to run, and took off. One of their safeties was coming up from his left and when Shawn saw that, he shifted the ball into his right hand. Small problem? As he did, a linebacker he *didn't* see came from Shawn's right and put his helmet directly on the football, like hitting a nail with a hammer.

Shawn didn't see him, didn't have a chance to hold on to the ball, it really was a direct hit. Ben watched the rest of it like it was happening in slow motion, like it was some weird sort of trick play. The ball popped straight up in the air, the safety who'd been running hard at Shawn from the left caught it in perfect stride.

Defense turning into offense that fast.

And the kid who had the ball now was *real* fast. Ben turned out to be the one with the best angle on him, did his best to get across the field and cut him off. But before he could try to cut him down he got leveled by a block from *his* blind side, laid out, Sam telling him when the play was over the block had been thrown by one of the Patriots' defensive ends.

There was nothing between the safety and the end zone after that except a lot of green grass. For the first time in the championship game, the Patriots were ahead. At least Sam managed to break up the conversion pass.

It was still Parkerville by six, 27-21.

"Told you I was feeling the pressure," Shawn said when they all got to the sideline, the refs deciding to give both teams a breather with an official time-out. "Different position, but same old Shawn."

Ben was about to tell him to forget it, there was way too much football to be played to start feeling sorry for himself, but Coach O'Brien was the one who spoke first, having overheard what his son just said.

He spoke to Ben, not Shawn.

"First play of the next series?" he said. "Throw that same hook again. Somebody showed me a couple of weeks ago that it's pure genius sometimes running the same play twice in a row."

Then walked away, Ben almost positive he heard him whistling.

On first down, Ben threw the same pass to Shawn, who clamped two hands on the ball, ran right over the safety who'd just scored the touchdown, ran fifteen yards after that. When he got back to the huddle Ben bumped him some fist and said, "Well, you were right about one thing."

"What?"

Ben shrugged and said, "Same guy."

The Rams then took it the rest of the way down the field. When they got to the Patriots twelve-yard line, Ben was supposed to look for Sam in the end zone. But the Patriots had Sam completely surrounded. There wasn't enough time for Ben — feeling surrounded himself — to look for anybody else, so he was forced to scramble, reversing his field, running hard to his left now.

A linebacker had him lined up, but Ben was still behind the line of scrimmage. So Ben brought the ball back up. Only he knew he was faking a throw to absolutely no one. But it froze the guy just enough, and in the next moment Ben was past him, sprinting for the orange pylon at the goal line, diving at the last second and putting the ball right on top of it like a cherry on a sundae — touchdown.

Darrelle was wide open in the corner on the conversion. Ben couldn't have missed him if he wanted to. Just like that it was 29-27, Rams, at The Rock.

Coach took Ben out for the kickoff, giving him a quick breather, even if it was for only one play. When Ben got to the sideline he got a quick drink of water, then allowed himself to look up into the stands to where he knew his parents and Lily were.

Jeff McBain was standing along with everybody else. When he saw Ben looking up at him, he just nodded, tapped his heart twice with his fist. Cheering quietly to the end. Ben's mom was holding her trusty video cam, always saying that recording the game made her less nervous.

Lily? It was as if she'd been waiting the whole game for Ben to look up at *her*. She smiled at Ben now, stepped forward just enough to show him she was wearing her favorite London T-shirt, from a trip she'd made there with her own parents last summer:

The one with "Big Ben" written over a picture of maybe the world's most famous clock.

The Rams forced the Patriots to punt on their next series after just three plays. Three and out. But the Rams couldn't move the ball, either, had to punt it right back after just one first down.

Suddenly it was if all the scoring in this game had worn down both teams at once, both defenses starting to dominate now the way the offenses had all afternoon.

With 3:30 showing on the clock, Patriots starting out on their own forty, Ben said to Sam, "You knew all day that the team with the ball last was gonna win."

"Means we need to get the ball back," Sam Brown said. "And then start running out the clock with it when we do."

"Sounds like a plan," Ben said.

Ben and Sam were back at safety, Coop at middle line-backer. The last few series Coach was even using Shawn as a rover back, lining him up with Coop sometimes, dropping him back into coverage, wanting all the size and speed in the game he could get, clearly.

In the defensive huddle, Ben looked around at his teammates and said, "You guys all know what the coach in *Friday Night Lights* said he meant by 'perfect,' right?"

Sam said, "Perfect isn't always about the score."

Coop said, "He said it was knowing you did all you could."

Ben said, "Let's be perfect now."

They all tried. Hard. Twice on the Patriots' drive they had Robbie Burnett looking at third and ten. Both times he completed the pass he needed to. Under a minute left, they had him at fourth and ten at the Rams' seventeen-yard line, and Coop seemed to have him down in the backfield. Somehow Robbie broke loose from Coop, kept his balance, broke what announcers always called the "contain" in football, ran two yards past the first-down chains and got out of bounds to stop the clock.

The last best chance they had to stop him was second and goal from the five. Robbie threw for Max Mahoney, his favorite receiver. But Sam cut in front of Max at the exact right moment, Ben was sure Sam was about to make one more hero play on defense. And if it had been a good throw, he would have had it. But it wasn't a good throw, or even close. Robbie threw high, way high, and that saved him, because even Sam couldn't jump high enough to get both hands on the ball.

Got one hand on it. That was all. Ball fell incomplete behind him. Sam dropped to his knees and pounding the ground like he wanted to break it when it did.

On the next play Robbie stepped back like he was going to throw again, but then pulled the ball down on a quarterback draw, ran up the middle and into the end zone untouched.

Twenty-five seconds left. Sam came all the way across the end zone to knock down Robbie's conversion pass to Max. In that moment, it still felt like too little, too late, even to Ben.

Patriots 33, Rams 29.

Just like that, everything changing that fast the way it always seemed to in sports, they had gone from winning to losing.

The Patriots didn't risk Ben breaking a long kickoff return on them, just squib-kicked the ball over midfield, where Coop was the one who fell on it, the clock stopping when he did.

Coach O'Brien gathered the guys on offense around him and said, "Listen, there's still time."

Nobody said anything, Ben wondering how many of the Rams actually believed him.

Ben just knowing that in that moment, even after what had just happened, *he* believed.

Looking at Ben, Coach O'Brien said, "What do you think?"

Ben said, "Coach, I figure we've got three plays left. To get to where I can throw it all the way into the end zone, we've got to be at their thirty."

"Okay," Coach said, "then here's what we're gonna do. What *you're* gonna do. We go to Shawn on the left sideline. If he catches it . . ." He waved his hands in front of him, like waving away his own words. "Sorry, I mean *when* he catches it, he gets right out of bounds. Then throw the same ball to Sam on the other side of the field, as far up the sideline as he can get. Then Sam gets out of bounds. We'll probably be inside ten seconds by then, so even with the clock stopped, I'll call a time-out." He grinned. "It will give me a little extra time to come up with something brilliant."

The linebacker on Shawn jammed him up coming off the line, but Shawn was big enough and strong enough to get past him, get on the kid's outside shoulder, get ten yards up the field and break to the sideline. As soon as he turned, the ball was there, Ben trusting it all the way. This time Shawn covered the ball with both arms like he was trying to hide it from everybody else on the field.

First down, Patriots' forty-two.

Twelve seconds left.

They didn't even huddle, everybody knew the next play they were going to run. Sam took off up the right sideline, like the Rams were going for it all right now, stopped and came back for the ball. Knowing it would be there, just because it always had been on McBain Field. It was now. Sam made the catch, took a quick look at the defense, knew that even with a time-out in Coach's pocket, he didn't want to run valuable seconds off the clock getting a few more yards.

Knowing they were on the thirty-one now, knowing they were close enough for Ben to get the ball in the end zone even if he was well back of the line of scrimmage.

Six seconds left.

Coach called his last time-out, waved Ben over to the sideline, a huge smile on his face.

"Maybe this is the way this crazy season is supposed to end," he said. "You know they're gonna double Sam. Probably triple him. And they'll most likely have everybody and their brothers strung out near the goal line. I figure that leaves Shawn with single coverage on the short side of the field, that same linebacker they've had on him. Shawn can beat him. And that's how we'll beat them."

"Okay," Ben McBain said, and then ran back to the huddle to run the last play of the football season.

"Hold your blocks," Ben said in the huddle after he gave the guys the play Coach had called. "That'll give me some time to run around and buy Shawn and the other receivers time to go deep."

Coop said, "Don't worry, nobody's sacking you."

Now Ben looked at Shawn. "You hug that sideline and run as fast and as far as you can."

"You sure you know what you're doing?" Shawn said.

"*Dude,*" Ben said. "Like, totally."

But as they broke the huddle, Ben ran over to Shawn, grabbed him by the shoulder, made sure he knew exactly how they were going to win the game.

How the story really *was* supposed to end.

Ben dropped back into the shotgun one more time. Before he called out the signals, he looked to his right, at Sam. His best bud in the world. Who didn't need to be told anything.

Sam nodded.

As soon as the ball was in Ben's hands, he ran to his right. Buying time, just like he said he would. Running to his right, dropping away from the line of scrimmage as he did. Giving the receivers enough time.

Now, he told himself.

Now he was running toward the line, coming forward, looking to his left. Looking for Shawn. Seeing that he had a step on the kid covering him.

Maybe two.

Bringing the ball up now, like he was going to throw it on the run, slowing just a little, his blockers having given him the room he needed to launch the ball.

The ball Ben McBain pulled back down now.

Faking it.

Then turning and looking straight down the field, to where he always knew he was going to throw it, to where he'd told Shawn he was going to throw it coming out of the huddle.

Throwing it to Sam Brown.

Ben saw that the fake had given Sam just enough of a chance to get behind everybody. Saw Sam run to the place in the middle of the end zone where he was always supposed to be. Where Phelan was that day against Miami when Flutie was doing what Ben was doing now, throwing it as far as he could to his best friend to win the big game.

Ben making the throw he'd always dreamed about making, being the quarterback he'd always dreamed about being.

Just as the ball was coming down out of the sky, he had to sidestep Coop, who was blocking his view. Like Ben had to avoid one of his own blockers so he could see the ball tracking on Sam like a missile tracking on a target in a video game.

Sam had turned and was facing him like a center fielder, facing the ball the way he always did when they'd practiced this play at McBain Field. Sam had always caught it there and caught it at The Rock now, caught it and just sat down in the end zone, holding the ball in his arms like he was already holding the championship trophy.

Ben ran and jumped his way down the field, pumping his arms above him as he did, like he was signaling touchdown over and over again, racing with the rest of his teammates trying to get to Sam Brown.

Sam was still in the end zone, somewhere underneath a pile of Rams that included Shawn and Justin and Darrelle. Ben ran for where they all were, just giving one quick look to the scoreboard, which showed there was no time left on the clock, or in this game, or in this season. All zeroes.

The only other numbers that mattered were these:

Home 35, Visitors 33.

When Sam finally managed to get up, he saw Ben standing in front of him.

"You knew I was coming to you," Ben said.

"We both knew."

Then he gave Ben a quick, smooth high five.

Ben grinned at him and said, "It's not like we haven't run that play a few times."

"Only our whole lives," Sam said.

Then Coop was there, helmet in hand already, looking about as happy as Ben had ever seen him. And Cooper Manley of the Core Four was always pretty happy to begin with, there really were no bad days for him.

"Well," he said, "that certainly didn't stink."

Shawn came walking over and said, "How did you ever make that throw?"

"Best reason in the world," Ben said. "I had to."

Shawn took his helmet off, wiped the sweat off his face as best as he could with the back of his hand. Just not the smile that stayed where it was.

"One more audible," he said. "Glad you told me."

"Figured the fewer people who knew, the better. But you needed to be one of them."

"It had to be Sam, didn't it?"

Ben said, "Yeah, it did."

Right before the trophy presentation, Coach O'Brien came over, pulled Ben aside, so it was just the two of them.

"I want you to know something," he said, "straight up. This was the best season I ever had in my life."

Ben said, "Mine, too, Coach." Then added, "Well, so far, anyway."

Coach pointed a finger at him now and said, "You changed my play."

"I guess I did."

In a quiet voice, Coach said, "You didn't trust Shawn?"

"Straight up, Coach? That had nothing to do with it. But it's like I told Shawn the other day: I always try to be the best teammate I can be. And I knew Sam was our best chance to win the game."

"You were right," Coach said.

Ben McBain laughed. "Good thing!" he said.

Coach walked away to get ready for the trophy presentation at midfield. That was when Ben saw Lily and his parents waving from behind the Rams' bench. Ben jogged over there.

His dad, as usual, hugged him first.

"Flutie to Phelan," he said.

"Or McBain to Brown, that's another way of looking at it now," Ben said to his dad.

"I thought I was only going to see that play once in my life," he said.

"Like you always tell me," Ben said. "Guy's open, you better get it to him."

"Even if you have to throw it as far as you can," Jeff McBain said.

"Are you kidding, Dad? I threw it *much* farther than that."

His mom hugged him then, held up her little recorder, said, "Now you can watch yourself make one of those Hail Mary passes you and your father are always going on and on about."

Ben's parents walked away. Him and Lily now at The Rock.

"Big Ben," she said.

"Not bad for a little guy, right?" he said.

She smiled. "Not bad at all," she said.

After the trophy presentation, it was decided that once everybody went home to change, they should all meet at Coach O'Brien's house for pizza and ice cream. But before they all left the field, there was one more presentation.

Coach came over to where Ben was standing with Sam and Coop and Lily, handed him the game ball.

"For making that throw," he said.

Ben immediately handed the ball to Sam, saying, "For making that catch."

Sam started to hand it back, saying, "No way."

So Coop grabbed the ball from both of them and said, "Why don't I just hold on to this for now and we'll work it out later."

"Genius," Ben said. "Hundred percent."

"I knew it!" Coop said.

Ben McBain took one last look out at the field, looked down to the end zone where Sam had made a catch he knew they would all remember forever, where he had made the kind of memory for all of them that Ben's dad said sports were supposed to make.

Then he turned back to his friends and, without saying a word, put his hand out in front of him, the way Coach did before every game.

Sam put his on top of it.

Coop and Lily did the same.

"Hey, can I get some of that?"

Shawn.

Ben answered, without hesitation.

"Get in here," he said.

Then Shawn's hand was on top of theirs. Just like that, they were five.

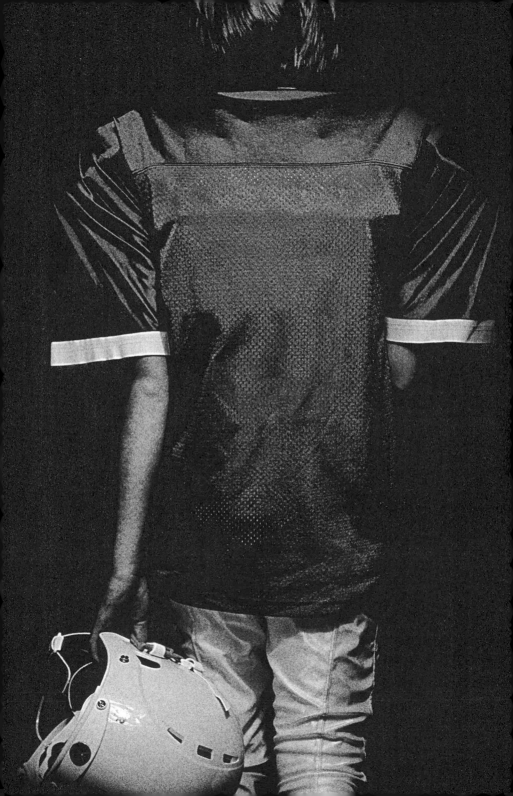

BASKETBALL **SE**ASON IS HERE. . . .

Ben, Sam, Coop, Shawn, and Lily return in a second Game Changers novel!

It's another sport — basketball — and a new season for Ben McBain and his friends. That means a new set of challenges, both on and off the court, for Ben, Sam, Coop, Shawn, and even Lily. Before the cheering has stopped at the end of the football season, their friendships will be tested at the tip-off of basketball season. Ben faces off against a new set of opponents and must come to terms with his own abilities in order to prove once again that it's not about getting knocked down in sports; it's about how you get back up afterward.

ACKNOWLEDGMENTS

To my wife, Taylor, and our four amazing children: Chris, Alex, Zach, and Hannah. They continue to make me want to be the best husband, the best father, the best writer of books like this one.